Bolan
lying on an operating table

A pair of green eyes peered at him from over a hospital face mask. Kristen Kemp sewed the last stitches into his shoulder and said, "You've lost a lot of blood."

"Where are we?" he asked.

"In my clinic."

Bolan sat up and tried to collect his thoughts. "How long was I out?" he asked.

"About an hour," she said.

Bolan remained silent, contemplating the likelihood that they'd been followed.

Kemp put her hands on Bolan's shoulders and tried to get him to lie back down. "You should rest."

"We're not safe here," Bolan said.

"Grassy Butte has two hundred and fifty people, and I know every last one of them. No one's going to harm us here," she said as she covered his wounds with sterile bandages.

"Whatever you thought you knew about this place changed the moment we got shot at yesterday," he told her. "Something big is going on here—and it's damned dangerous."

Before Kemp could respond, Bolan saw the shadow of a man holding what could only be a gun outlined in the window. He grabbed Kemp's shoulders and flipped her over him, as automatic gunfire tore through the walls of the clinic.

Hurling himself on top of her, Bolan had just one more question. "Where are my weapons?"

MACK BOLAN ®
The Executioner

The Executioner
Don Pendleton's
TOXIC TERRAIN

A GOLD EAGLE BOOK FROM

WORLDWIDE®

TORONTO • NEW YORK • LONDON
AMSTERDAM • PARIS • SYDNEY • HAMBURG
STOCKHOLM • ATHENS • TOKYO • MILAN
MADRID • WARSAW • BUDAPEST • AUCKLAND

Recycling programs
for this product may
not exist in your area.

First edition May 2011

ISBN-13: 978-0-373-64390-5

Special thanks and acknowledgment to
Darwin Holmstrom for his contribution to this work.

TOXIC TERRAIN

Printed in U.S.A.

Hesitation and half measures lose all in war.

—Napoleon Bonaparte
1769–1821
Napoleon I: Maxims of War

A threat against America is a threat against me—and I will not hesitate to take out all conspirators, with swiftness and finality.

—Mack Bolan

THE
MACK BOLAN
LEGEND

Nothing less than a war could have fashioned the destiny of the man called Mack Bolan. Bolan earned the Executioner title in the jungle hell of Vietnam.

But this soldier also wore another name—Sergeant Mercy. He was so tagged because of the compassion he showed to wounded comrades-in-arms and Vietnamese civilians.

Mack Bolan's second tour of duty ended prematurely when he was given emergency leave to return home and bury his family, victims of the Mob. Then he declared a one-man war against the Mafia.

He confronted the Families head-on from coast to coast, and soon a hope of victory began to appear. But Bolan had broken society's every rule. That same society started gunning for this elusive warrior—to no avail.

So Bolan was offered amnesty to work within the system against terrorism. This time, as an employee of Uncle Sam, Bolan became Colonel John Phoenix. With a command center at Stony Man Farm in Virginia, he and his new allies—Able Team and Phoenix Force—waged relentless war on a new adversary: the KGB.

But when his one true love, April Rose, died at the hands of the Soviet terror machine, Bolan severed all ties with Establishment authority.

Now, after a lengthy lone-wolf struggle and much soul-searching, the Executioner has agreed to enter an "arm's-length" alliance with his government once more, reserving the right to pursue personal missions in his Everlasting War.

Prologue

Grassy Butte, North Dakota

Pam Bowman stared down at the dead Hereford calf at her feet and said, "This is not good."

"It most certainly is not," the man standing next to her confirmed.

He would know, Bowman thought. Though he was just the McKenzie County extension agent, Roger Grevoy had earned both an M.D. and a Ph.D. from Johns Hopkins, and had at one time been considered among the world's top researchers studying the pathology of communicable diseases. Grevoy had never discussed how he'd gone from holding a high-powered research job with the Pentagon to being a lowly county extension agent, but Bowman suspected it had something to do with the meetings he went to in the basement of the local Catholic church every Wednesday night. Whatever the reason, she was damned glad to have his help.

"Is it what I think it is?" Bowman asked.

"I won't have the test results until tomorrow," Grevoy

said, "but it looks like it might be. I've seen it before. Bovine spongiform encephalopathy. Mad cow disease."

"How's that possible?" Bowman asked. "This calf can't be but four months old. It takes years for an animal to die from BSE."

"I know. I think we're dealing with something we've never seen before. And it's extremely bad."

"We'd better start riding back to the truck if we're going to get out of here before sunset," Bowman said.

Grevoy packed his tissue samples in the dry-ice packs in his saddlebag and the pair mounted their horses. They had ridden nearly an hour to get to the infected herd and had about fifty minutes before the sun set. They had good horses, but even a healthy, strong horse would have a difficult time negotiating the North Dakota Badlands in the dark.

They hadn't ridden fifteen minutes before they heard the "whoop-whoop-whoop" of helicopter blades breaking the near silence that usually blanketed the rough country. On rare occasions one of the oil companies with wells in the Badlands would fly a helicopter out to a drill site, but not often because the bizarre rugged terrain of the area, with its deep crevasses and gullies carved out of the soft bentonite clay soil, offered few places to land a helicopter. Bowman's grandfather had once described the Badlands as "mountains that go down into the earth instead of up out of it."

The helicopter skimmed over the top of a butte and hovered about twenty feet above the trail. The horses Grevoy and Bowman rode were strong and sure of foot—they weren't easily spooked and wouldn't get upset over anything as mundane as a rattlesnake or a mountain lion. But they were not used to helicopters, and Grevoy's horse reared up, tossing him to the ground. Ropes fell from the

helicopter, and armed men clad in black combat gear slid
down to the ground. Bowman reached for the .338 Marlin
Express in her saddle scabbard, but before she could pull
the lever-action carbine free of its leather, the armed men
had combat rifles pointed at both her and Grevoy.

Several pairs of hands pulled Bowman off her horse
and threw her face-first to the ground. She looked over
and saw Grevoy trying to fight back. One of the men
smashed the butt of his collapsible rifle stock into Grevoy's head, knocking him unconscious. A couple of men
tied Bowman's hands behind her back and bound her feet
together. The last thing she saw before they put the hood
over her head was a group of men removing the saddles
and bridles from their horses and setting the animals free.
Anyone who saw them would assume they were wild
horses that had strayed outside the confines of Theodore Roosevelt National Park, at least until they got close
enough to see the brands. Then she felt a thud on the back
of her head and the lights went out.

1

The beauty of the North Dakota Badlands surrounded Mack Bolan as he rode across the terrain on horseback, following Dr. Kristen Kemp, co-owner of a large-animal veterinary clinic in Grassy Butte. Her partner, Pam Bowman, had disappeared a few days earlier, along with Roger Grevoy, a former Pentagon researcher who specialized in communicable diseases.

Grevoy had done some work for Stony Man Farm, an intelligence organization that operated so far under the radar that only the President of the United States and a select few knew of its existence. Grevoy's drinking had eventually destroyed his once-promising career and taken over his life.

The last Bolan had heard, Grevoy was getting back on track. He had several years of sobriety and had been rebuilding his relationship with his ex-wife and kids. When Grevoy disappeared, his ex-wife had contacted Hal Brognola, director of the Sensitive Operations Group, based at Stony Man Farm, and asked for his help, which was how the Executioner found himself riding a horse through the North Dakota Badlands, with the comely large-animal veterinarian riding the horse in front of him.

Suddenly Kemp stopped her horse at the beginning of a tree-lined ravine. "They found Pam's horse in this wooded draw. Its saddle and bridle were gone. They haven't found Rog's horse yet."

"What were they doing out here?"

"I'm not sure." Bolan got the sense Kemp was holding back on him, but he said nothing.

"What do you do again, Mr. Cooper? And why are you out here?"

Bolan repeated his cover story, that he was Matt Cooper, a security consultant who'd worked with Grevoy on a government contract when the man had been with the Department of Defense. The two had become friends, and he was here at the request of Grevoy's family. The details were vague enough to raise Kemp's suspicions.

"So what, exactly, is a 'security consultant'?" she asked, examining the Executioner's face.

"I'm an expert on securing things."

"How about killing things?" Kemp asked.

"Sometimes that's part of the job." The woman seemed about to respond—she struck Bolan as someone who liked to have the last word—but before any sound could leave her lips the crack of a rifle split the air and a crater erupted in the trunk of a Rocky Mountain juniper tree just inches from her head.

"Get down," Bolan shouted. He'd already pulled his gun from the scabbard, a DPMS LR-260L, an AR-10-type rifle chambered for the .260 Remington round, and pulled Kemp off her horse. He noted that she'd grabbed her Marlin 1895G Guide carbine from its scabbard. She was nearly down when a second round hit her horse and it fell on top of the vet, pinning her leg to the ground.

"You okay?" Bolan asked.

"I think so, but my foot's caught in the stirrup."

Bolan looked for something to use for a lever but found nothing better than the rifle in Kemp's hands. Unfazed by the rounds that continued to hit the dead horse providing cover between them and the shooter, Bolan lowered the hammer to the half-cocked position and wedged the stock in between the horse's carcass and the ground, as close as he could get to Kemp's leg, and tried to lift the dead animal. He managed to get enough space for the woman to work her foot free. They crawled away from the horse, keeping out of range from the rifle shots that flew over their heads. The rough terrain provided the pair with cover from their would-be assassin—or assassins—and they made it into the temporary safety of the wooded draw.

Bolan checked Kemp's leg, which was already showing bruises but didn't seem broken. "You're bleeding," he said, wiping a trickle of blood from her cheek.

"I think I got hit with slivers from the juniper."

"Stay down," he told her. "I saw where the shooter's hiding. I'm going to try to get a shot at him." Bolan crept along a low wash in the draw, which would have been a streambed in those few times of the year when the arid Badlands had measurable precipitation. He reached an outcropping near the end of the draw, edged his rifle between a couple of boulders and peered through the Nikon Laser IRT scope. He made out the top of a desert-camo boonie hat poking over a ridge exactly 436 yards to the southeast, according to the scope's built-in range finder. He placed the crosshairs of his reticle on the part of the boonie hat that would contain at least a portion of the wearer's head, and squeezed off a round.

It was an easy shot and Bolan watched the shooter's

cap disappear, along with a good chunk of the back of his head, judging by the red spray that went with it. The soldier watched for other signs of movement from behind the ridge, waiting several minutes before he moved from his hide.

Meanwhile, Kemp had worked her way along the wash and joined him. "I told you to stay back," he told her.

"You told me to stay down. I stayed down. Besides, I don't recall signing the contract that made you the boss of me. Did you get him?"

"I think so. I'm waiting to see if there's anyone else out there." Kemp took off her cowboy hat and flung it Frisbee-style into the open. Nothing happened.

Bolan checked out Kemp's firearm. The Marlin 1895G Guide was a good choice for the sort of work she was likely to need it for—stray buffalo, hormone-crazed Angus bulls, maybe an elk, a stray cougar, or even a bear—but it made a lousy sniper rifle. It fired the slow-but-hard-hitting .45-70 Government round, making it ideal for big game in close quarters, but practically useless at 400-plus yards.

"You familiar with an AR?" he asked her.

"I paid my way through college by serving in the military," she said. "It's been a while, but I could still field-strip that thing down to the firing pin."

He handed her the DPMS and took the Marlin. "Cover me. I'm going to sneak around the ridge and make my way up to the shooter. If you see anything moving that's not me, shoot it."

Using the terrain and flora for cover, Bolan made his way to the back of the ridge. Using a pair of compact binoculars, he scanned the area for other potential shooters but saw nothing other than a horse tethered to some brush at the base of the ridge opposite the gully where he'd left

Kemp. He made his way up the ridge and found the shooter's body slumped over an old, dry log, the back of his head blown away.

When Kemp saw Bolan standing on the ridge, she jogged over and climbed to the top. Bolan had turned the body over and retrieved a wallet from the back pocket of the jeans. The vet looked at the shooter's face and Bolan asked, "Know him?"

"Not really. I've seen him in town once or twice, but he's not from around here. He works for Ag Con." She looked at the bloody corpse. "He *worked* for Ag Con," she corrected herself.

"Agricultural Conglomerates?" Bolan asked.

"Yeah, they're the biggest employer in the county. Hell, in this half of the state. They must have three or four hundred employees, but they don't hire any locals."

"You or Ms. Bowman ever do any work for them?"

"Not directly. They have their own vets on staff."

"Ever do anything for them indirectly?" Bolan asked. Once again he sensed that she was holding out on him.

Kemp looked him up and down. "Don't take this the wrong way," she said, "but when it comes to Ag Con, we've developed the habit of watching what we say around here. They've been known to bring in a few 'security consultants' of their own. Near as I can tell, you just saved my life—maybe, maybe not. How can I be one hundred percent sure I can trust you?"

Bolan looked straight into Kemp's sparkling green eyes. "You can't," he replied. "How can you be one hundred percent sure about anything?"

"You can't."

"Sometimes you just have to believe what your gut tells you," Bolan said.

"Is that one of your security-consultant aphorisms?"

"Yep. Aphorism number seventeen. Want to hear one through sixteen?"

"No, thanks," she replied. "One's enough for the time being."

Then it was her turn to stare into the eyes of the man who'd introduced himself as "Matt Cooper." When she looked into his icy blue eyes, she felt trust. "At least you weren't the guy who shot my horse. That's something, I guess."

"If it helps, I'll be as honest as I can about who I am and what I'm doing here," Bolan said. "You've probably figured out that there's a reason I can't be more specific. But what I can tell you is that I intend to find out what happened to Rog and Ms. Bowman and hopefully bring them home safely. I have some training and experience in this sort of thing.

"I should also tell you that I know Rog and Bowman were investigating a possible outbreak of BSE," Bolan continued. "Rog suspected that the prions that cause BSE had in some ways mutated, and that had him worried."

"So why'd you need me to tell you about that?" Kemp asked.

"You're not the only one who needs to know who can and can't be trusted."

"Do you already know about Ag Con, too?"

"Some. It's Chinese-owned, but the exact nature of the corporation is a little murky." He didn't tell her that Stony Man Farm intelligence indicated Ag Con was controlled by retired officers of the People's Liberation Army— PLA—and ranking members of the Central Military Commission of the Communist Party of China. Aaron "the Bear" Kurtzman, who headed Stony Man Farm's team of crack cybersleuths, was helping Bolan on this project. He had become friends with Roger Grevoy and wanted to find out what happened to the man. Kurtzman suspected that some of the Ag Con's principal owners were part of a secret cabal dedicated to ending China's drive toward a free-market economy and restoring the country's former socialist status quo by creating chaos in China's primary export market: the United States. This was just a suspicion on Kurtzman's part; since he and his team hadn't been able to find any substantial evidence about the existence of this cabal. But it was starting to look as though Bolan might have found a solid lead.

Bolan didn't withhold this because of lack of trust in Kemp—his gut was telling him she was okay, and he tended to take his own advice. He withheld it because at this point it wasn't solid information but rather innuendo and rumor based on vague suspicion.

"What do you know about me?" Kemp asked.

"You're thirty-four, you have a doctorate in veterinary medicine from Purdue University, you served six years in the military, where you finished your undergraduate degree and started your doctoral program, you have far too many speeding tickets, and you are the co-owner of Grassy Butte Veterinary Clinic with Ms. Bowman."

"Anything else?"

"You and Ms. Bowman are lovers."

"My, you are thorough," Kemp said. "But not completely up-to-date. We were lovers, not that it's any of your business. These days Pam and I are just business partners again. She's got another partner in her personal life."

"You okay with that?"

"You mean did I kill her in a jealous rage? Who the hell are you again? Wait, I know—Matt Cooper, security consultant. I guess you got me. I busted a cap in both her and Rog's asses because I couldn't stand the thought of her with another chick." She held out her hands. "You might as well cuff me and bring me in."

Kemp was a tiny woman, maybe five-two in her stockings, tops, but she had an energy that seemed much larger, and Bolan couldn't help but like the incendiary little brunette. He could see the gold flecks in her green irises start to glow, but she calmed down.

"Sorry if I got a little melodramatic," she said. "I'm not used to complete strangers regaling me with the sordid details of my love life, especially while I'm standing over the dead body of another stranger who just tried to kill me."

"About that," Bolan said. "I suppose we have to call the sheriff. Can we trust him?"

"Jim Buck? Hell, yes, we can trust him—to a point, anyway. I know he's not working for Ag Con, though he does have to answer to some county commissioners who do. Plus he's as lazy as they come. He's not going to be happy with all the paperwork this is going to create."

"I have to say, you're taking this dead body thing fairly well."

Kemp looked down at the corpse. "I put down animals all the time," she said, "and most of them have never done anything to me. This son of a bitch shot my favorite horse. Please excuse my lack of compassion."

Watford City, North Dakota

"SHUT THE FUCK UP," Gordon Gould said to the large man standing in his office. "I'm trying to think." McKenzie County Sheriff Jim Buck didn't appreciate being treated in that manner, but Gould, president of the North Dakota Cattle Raisers' Association—and one of the most powerful men in the state—could make Jim Buck's life a living hell.

After he'd digested the information Buck had given him, Gould said, "Tell me again what happened."

"Apparently one of those guys Ag Con brought in from out of state went ape shit and tried to shoot Kristen Kemp and some dude named Cooper up north of Beicegel Creek Road, just east of the Little Missouri River."

"So how come the guy from Ag Con is dead instead of that woman or her friend?"

"I guess he missed and shot Kemp's horse," Buck said.

"So you're just taking her word for this?" Gould said.

"Her word and the word of Cooper, the guy who was with her."

"Who the fuck is he?"

"I checked him out. He's a retired Marine, lists his current occupation as 'security consultant.' Seems to have some pull with Justice and his record's spotless." As usual, Kurtzman had done an outstanding job setting up Bolan's cover identity.

"Besides," Buck said, "all the evidence backs up their story. The Ag Con guy fired four shots into the wooded draw where Kemp and Cooper were riding their horses. He was either poaching and thought the horses were elk, in which case he was even blinder than he was stupid, or the man was trying to kill them, which is what I'd say it looks like he was trying to do."

"You're going to write it up as an accident," Gould said.

"What the hell are you talking about?" Buck asked.

"I said you're going to write it up as an accident. The man was out poaching, mistook the horses for elk and forced Cooper to return fire."

"I'll do no such thing. That's pure bullshit, and you know it."

"I also know that I have evidence that Linda's been stealing meth from the evidence room and selling it to support her casino habit."

"You're full of shit." Linda was Buck's wife. The sheriff knew she had a gambling problem, but he couldn't believe she'd sink that low.

"I figured you'd see it that way," Gould said and pulled a remote control from his desk drawer. A large LCD monitor on the wall beeped and came to life. "In case you get any ideas, I burned these disks from the originals, which are now in the possession of my lawyer. Watch."

He hit Play and a grainy image of Linda Buck appeared on the screen. The DVD was obviously taken with the security camera in the sheriff department's evidence room. Buck watched as his wife, who happened to be the legal secretary for the county attorney, walked into the room and removed a package containing at least an ounce of meth. Gould stopped the DVD, and Buck heard the tray in the multidisk DVD player rotate. Gould hit Play again, and once more Linda appeared on screen. This time the camera appeared to be at a low angle in the cab of a pickup truck. The wide-angle lens showed Linda handing the package of meth to a fellow Buck recognized as Gould's nephew, Jason. In return the nephew handed her a large envelope. Linda pulled a large stack of bills from the envelope and counted them. She was an attractive woman, in spite of her 1970s-era Farrah Fawcett hairdo. When she finished counting the money, Jason said something Buck couldn't quite make out and then started to unzip his pants. Once he'd exposed himself, Linda moved toward his lap.

"Do you want to see the rest?" Gould asked.

"I've seen enough," Buck said and Gould stopped the DVD.

"Isn't that the mother of your children?" Gould asked.

Buck didn't respond. He had his head in his hands and his shoulders shook. The sheriff was crying.

"Look," Gould said. "I know you feel like killing me. I know you feel like killing her. But where will your kids be if their mamma's dead and their daddy's in prison for killing her? Don't be mad at her. Gambling is a powerful addiction. Wouldn't it just be easier to fill out the report the way I tell you to fill it out? Take care of this issue for me, then you get her the help she needs. I'll even pay for it."

WHEN BOLAN WAS four miles from Ag Con's main complex in Trotters, North Dakota, he tethered his horse to a juniper in a deep wash where the animal wouldn't be seen unless an aircraft flew directly over it. The satellite intel he'd received from Stony Man Farm had been sketchy—there weren't a lot of satellites readily available to look at this remote part of the world, since it wasn't exactly a high-priority hot spot for any of the world's intelligence agencies—but from what he'd seen, the complex, which consisted of corrugated-steel pole buildings and an old ranch house that had been converted into office space, as well as a few barns and other outbuildings left over from the complex's previous life as a working ranch, appeared to be patrolled by armed guards.

Bolan was armed with his rifle, which he wore from a three-point sling so he could access it while riding, as well as his .44 Magnum Desert Eagle and his silenced Beretta 93-R machine pistol. But this was a soft probe, and Bolan had no intention of shedding any blood on this excursion. Even though he didn't buy the sheriff's conclusion about that morning's shooting being an accident, he had no hard evidence that the shooter had been acting on orders from his employer. The Executioner had no qualms about doling out judgment on the guilty, but he drew the line at murdering the innocent, and the Ag Con employees were innocent until he knew for certain that was not the case.

When he was within one thousand yards of the complex, he made his way to the top of the highest butte he could find. It was mid-July and most of the accessible grass had been grazed by this time of year, but not even the heartiest Badlands cattle could have made their way up the steep slopes of the butte. The grass at the top, though sparse, was tall and provided good cover. Bolan crawled through the grass to the edge of the butte nearest the compound and scanned the complex with a pair of 18-power binoculars that were the next best thing to being there. He identified four men carrying rifles patrolling the perimeter on quads. Inside the fence he counted at least four more armed patrols on the ground. An old hip-roof barn appeared to have been converted into office space or sleeping quarters; its windows had been recently replaced, and an industrial-size air-conditioning unit cooled the building. Bolan noted that there was an additional window-style air-conditioning unit mounted in the over-size cupola atop the barn. On closer examination, Bolan saw that the cupola was air-conditioned for the comfort of the armed guard posted inside. Several other armed guards were stationed around the barn itself.

The level of security was nothing short of bizarre. Most cattle operations in the area needed only the security of a big dog or perhaps some alpacas to keep coyotes and other predators away from the calves. Even though the Little Missouri National Grasslands—a chunk of land that covered more than a million acres in western North

Dakota—was all open-grazing, meaning the cattle roamed on more or less free range, most ranchers kept their herds together and they knew one another's brands and tags. The closest anyone ever got to rustling was when a stray animal accidentally ended up in someone else's herd, and those situations were usually solved with no hard feelings. Though most people out here carried at least one firearm at all times, and often two, that had more to do with the chance of running into a rattlesnake or buffalo that had strayed from Theodore Roosevelt National Park, or a rogue Angus or Hereford, than with fear of humans.

A Bell 210 helicopter flew over the river and landed in the complex just as the sun sank below the western horizon. Except for the yellow-and-red "Ag Con" decal on its side, the 210 was painted flat black. The first helicopter had barely landed when a second came in from the north. Again, while unusual, Ag Con's flying a couple of helicopters out here wasn't unreasonable. The company ran twenty thousand head of cattle in a range that covered over more than sixteen hundred square miles. It would be a challenge to cover it all on ATVs and horses.

But the men wearing full battle gear inside the helicopters were a little harder to explain. Bolan had a hard time imagining a legitimate use for the grenade launchers mounted beneath their QBZ Type 97 assault rifles. Grenades weren't the most useful tools for rounding up cattle or mending fences. The rifles themselves, modern bullpup-style weapons, with their grenade launchers poking out from under their barrels, looked as out of place in the Western landscape. Not to mention that the Type 97 had never been legally imported into the United States.

Several other men came out of the guarded barn dragging something that eliminated any doubts Bolan might have still harbored regarding the nature of the Ag Con operation—two figures, a male and a female, both with their hands and feet zip-tied together and black hoods draped over their heads. They had to be Pam Bowman and Roger Grevoy. Seeing the two captives was all the evidence Bolan needed to turn this into a shooting war.

Though he was well-armed, the Executioner could see no way to turn this soft probe hard without endangering the captives. Bolan had taken on more people than were guarding the compound and lived to tell about it, but if he started shooting now, there was no way he could take out all the enemy before they executed Bowman and Grevoy.

He watched as the prisoners were loaded onto one of the helicopters and flown from the compound. The Bell had a maximum range of 225 nautical miles, but since it hadn't refueled, its destination was likely much less than that. The helicopter headed northeast and was soon followed by the second helicopter. There was no cell phone service this far into the Badlands, but Bolan had brought a satellite phone in case he needed some help from Stony Man. Bolan punched in Kurtzman's secure number, but before he heard the big man's gruff voice answer, he felt a gun barrel touch the back of his head.

"Put down the phone," a voice behind him said.

Bolan, still in a prone position, started to put the phone down in an exaggerated slow-motion movement. Hoping that the man's attention was on his arm, the soldier swept his leg around behind him where he estimated the man would be standing. His calf hooking around the other man's leg told the soldier that he had guessed correctly, and the man fell to the ground. Bolan felt the barrel of the gun slide away from the back of his head at the same time he felt the man fall. The man squeezed the trigger an instant after the tip of the barrel left the back of Bolan's scalp and he felt a hot line sear across the back of his head. The bullet didn't hit him with enough force to cause any concussive damage, but the report from the rifle deafened the soldier—all he could hear was loud ringing.

But he didn't have time to worry about any permanent hearing loss. He flipped upright and drew his Desert Eagle before the man hit the ground. There was no point bothering with the silenced Beretta, since the soft probe had already gone hard. Bolan aimed and fired. The big 240-grain bullet put a crater the size of a walnut in the man's forehead and took half his skull with it on the way out.

Bolan still couldn't hear anything but ringing, but he knew the bad guys would be coming at him in force. He rolled back over and scanned the compound. By this time the sun had gone below the horizon, so he turned on the FLIR thermal imaging sight he'd mounted on the DPMS rifle. Sure enough, all four ATV riders were headed his way, as were a number of foot patrols from inside the compound. Bolan fired a shot at the ATV rider nearest the butte, hitting him in the gap between his full-coverage helmet and the chest protector of his motocross body armor. The .260 round would easily punch through the ABS plastic of the man's riding gear, but Bolan, who was used to fighting foes wearing antiballistic body armor rather than protective riding gear, instinctively aimed for open flesh. His shot was dead-on and a gaping wound opened in the man's trachea. The bullet sheared the man's spine just below the base of the skull, and he tumbled from his vehicle.

Before the man hit the ground, Bolan had already fired on the ATV rider who was next in line. He didn't have a clear shot at the man's neck, so he punched a round through the man's goggles.

The two ATV riders who were behind their fallen

comrades both reacted in different ways. The rider who was farther back stopped and tried to get behind his vehicle for cover, while the closer rider opened up his throttle and came bouncing toward Bolan at top speed. The soldier put a round right into the armpit of the man who was clambering off his ATV, and the guy fell from sight. Then Bolan targeted the rider coming at him on the ATV. It took two shots to stop him. Since he was so close to the butte, Bolan had to shoot almost straight down at him, taking him out with a shot through the top of his helmet.

All of this took place in a matter of seconds, but it was long enough for the shooter in the cupola atop the barn to start firing at Bolan's position. Bullets started knocking up chunks of dirt all around the Executioner, and at least a dozen armed men had left the compound and were running toward him. Bolan scooped up the sat phone, scrambled back to the far edge of the butte and leaped over the edge, half falling, half running down the steep embankment. When he reached the bottom he ran toward his horse. He knew the terrain would be too rough for anything but foot travel or horseback, so he ran at top speed through the bottoms of the maze of washes and gullies that made up the Badlands, knowing that he could keep ahead of the Ag Con goons.

The ringing in Bolan's ears had finally subsided. He regained his hearing just in time; voices in the brush ahead told Bolan that he also had to worry about what was in front of him as well as what was coming up behind. He could make out two distinct voices speaking with each other in the far end of the wash. He was still a good mile from his horse.

As quietly as he could, the soldier climbed to the top of the wash and took cover in a shrubby growth of juniper trees. From his vantage point he could see four armed

men through his FLIR sight. A quick scan in the other direction showed Bolan that the armed men from the compound who were spread out and combing the area looking
for him were closing in.

He pulled a pin from an M-67 fragmentation grenade
and lobbed the bomb toward the men in the wash, then
ducked behind a pile of rocks and clay. Though he was
out of the kill radius of the grenade, he was still close
enough to be wounded by flying shrapnel.

One of the men in the wash had time to utter, "What
the…" just before the grenade detonated. Bolan also heard
the sound of other guards coming down the path he'd just
made through the shrubs, but before he could identify
his trackers, the bomb went off. When the Executioner
scanned for survivors after the blast, all he saw was the
brightly colored thermal signatures of a leg and a couple
of arms amid the less brightly colored signature of the
bloody mist that was all that remained of the four men.

He did make out another five-man patrol heading
toward the sound of the explosion. Bolan once again broke
into a full-speed run through the rough terrain and made
it to his horse. He didn't take time to scan for his pursuers
with the FLIR, but he hoped they were still combing the
area and not making nearly as good time as he was. Bolan
untied the horse and led it out of the draw as quietly as
possible. After about a quarter mile he reached the trail
he rode in on. He could hear his pursuers closing in by the
time he mounted the horse and gave it his heels. The horse
broke into a run just as a man emerged from a stand of
junipers at the rim of a ridge that ran parallel to the trail.
The gunner fired a full-auto burst at the fleeing soldier,
but Bolan had already put enough distance between them

for the shots to fall short. The horse was given its lead and it ran until Bolan was certain he'd gotten far enough away from his pursuers.

2

Chen Zhen erupted from the barn door before the report from the first shot had quit echoing off the distant buttes. He watched as the ATV-mounted patrols were mowed down as they descended on the shooter's position on the butte to the east of the ranch. They were supposed to be good—they'd chosen Build & Berg Associates because of their reputation as the best private military contractor available—but so far they hadn't impressed Chen as especially competent.

At least he had his own men upon which he could depend, troops handpicked from among the very best the People's Liberation Army had to offer, and Yao Rui, the sharpshooter manning the cupola, had been one of the PLA's finest snipers. Before Chen could make out the exact location of the shots coming from the butte, he heard Yao's Barrett M-98 unleash several rounds. The booming of the powerful .338 Lapua Magnum rounds rang through the Badlands like the sonic boom from a jet fighter, but Chen couldn't see any sign that they'd hit their target.

Chen grabbed the radio clipped to his belt, pressed the talk button and heard the voice of Colonel Liang Wu, his associate who oversaw the PLA contingent and acted as his liaison with B&B Associates. Chen's English was rudimentary at best, while Liang was fluent in not only English, but also Russian and French, as well as several of the other languages spoken by the eclectic collection of mercenaries that comprised the B&B contingent.

"Find out what's happening," Chen ordered, "and report back to me the instant you have information."

Chen had no idea who was trespassing on Ag Con property, but at least he knew who it wasn't. Chen knew Ag Con had nothing to fear from the authorities. Gordon Gould had assured him that he would take care of officials from the local law-enforcement agency, which consisted of that fat buffoon Jim Buck and his simpleminded deputies. Likewise Governor Chauvin had given his assurance that Ag Con could count on nothing but the utmost support from the state highway-patrol department. Ag Con was the state's largest employer and had single-handedly kept North Dakota's economy growing throughout the United States' most recent economic turmoil.

Chauvin, who had his sights set on a seat in the U.S. Senate, was not about to let anything like a criminal investigation get in the way of commerce or his political future. Ag Con supplied the butter that Chauvin put upon his bread. Chen knew that wasn't the exact translation for the American idiomatic expression, but he knew it was close. Chauvin aspired to a higher office, and for that to happen, he needed the campaign funding that Ag Con provided. That's how things worked in a so-called democracy, Chen thought. In his opinion the word seemed to be code for a system of political prostitution, in which an oligarchy of corporate pimps like Ag Con ran a stable of political whores like Chauvin. To keep this illusion of democracy alive, the political whores spouted rhetoric

designed to appease one political faction or another. They
seemed to focus on emotionally charged but ultimately
meaningless issues to keep their constituency distracted
from the real matter at hand, which appeared to be finan-
cially raping the population.

Chen had spent much time with Governor Chauvin,
and he wasn't convinced the governor would have spurned
Ag Con's financial resources even if he had known the
corporation's real motive, which was nothing less than the
complete destabilization of the U.S. economy. Chauvin
most likely would win his seat in the U.S. Senate, but by
the time that occurred, the Senate would not have a stable
civilization to govern. Chen wasn't sure that Chauvin
possessed the intellectual tools to comprehend Ag Con's
plans even if he knew of them. If their plans were success-
ful—*when,* not *if,* Chen reminded himself—the United
States would devolve into societal chaos that would make
countries like Somalia and Haiti seem stable.

Regardless of whether or not he had the intelligence
to comprehend such possibilities, Chauvin had effectively
removed the state police from the equation. That left the
Bureau of Criminal Investigation, which answered not to
Chauvin but to North Dakota's attorney general, Jack Pullman. They were even less a threat than the highway patrol
because Gould had video footage of Pullman having sex
with a prostitute. When confronted with evidence of his
illicit activity, Pullman had been willing to make any
compromise in order to keep his secret safe.

When it came to doing business in North Dakota, Ag
Con was above the law, meaning that the intruder killing
his men from atop the butte was something other than of-
ficial. Most likely it had something to do with the abduc-
tion of the extension agent and the veterinarian.

Chen watched Liang and a small patrol of his men race

away from the compound on foot. This new development worried him. He hadn't expected to encounter any resistance this early in the process, but he had complete faith in Liang and his ability to neutralize the resistance.

LIANG AND HIS MEN raced around the butte and caught a glimpse of a dark figure disappearing into the sagebrush. He signaled for his men to stop and listen to the fleeing figure. Liang could hear the sound of the man cutting through the sagebrush, but he was remarkably quiet. He had no idea who he and his men were up against, but he was certain of one thing—the man was a professional.

But so were Liang and his troops, and once he'd identified the direction in which his prey was headed, they broke into a full run and pursued him. They moved through the brush almost as stealthily as the big man they tracked. Almost, but not quite.

Liang sensed they were getting close, and he knew beyond a shadow of a doubt they were on the right track when he heard the grenade go off. The terrain made progress difficult, but when they heard the explosion, Liang and his men moved even faster, until they came into a clearing awash in blood and dismembered body parts. Equine carnage mixed with the human gore; the Build & Berg mercenaries had ridden to the site on horseback, and two of the four horses had been killed in the explosion. A third had been severely wounded by shrapnel and would soon expire, but the fourth appeared relatively unharmed, perhaps because it had been shielded from the blast by the other horses.

Liang heard movement on the ridge above the massacre site. "After him!" he ordered his men. The men took off after the intruder in an instant, exhibiting the discipline that Liang had spent years instilling in them. Meanwhile, he untied and mounted the surviving horse.

Liang felt at home atop the horse. Mongol blood coursed through his veins, a shameful family secret that he'd managed to keep from his superiors, but at the same time a source of inner pride. Liang always felt that his secret Mongol heritage made him the fierce warrior he was. He'd definitely inherited his ability to ride a horse from his Mongolian ancestors.

Liang crouched low on the horse to avoid being swept from the saddle by the juniper branches and rode through the bottom of the gully toward the sound of the reports issuing from his troops' rifles. He couldn't hear any return fire and hoped that meant that their bullets had found their intended target. He burst out of the gully just as the horseback-mounted figure disappeared into the fading twilight. It appeared as though the man had not been wounded in the exchange of fire.

Liang estimated the distance between himself and the fleeing figure. Setting his selector to single-round fire, he sighted in on the man, then raised his sights to account for what he'd heard the American Southerners refer to as "Kentucky windage." He carefully squeezed off a shot. By the time he brought his rifle down and peered at the fleeing figure through the light-amplifying scope he'd mounted atop it, the target was slumped over in his saddle.

There was no time to congratulate himself on his lucky shot. Liang gave the horse his heels and charged toward the fleeing figure. All things being equal, he thought he should be able to catch the man. Both the intruder and he were mounted on quarter horses with similar musculature, but the big man he chased had to weigh at least 200 pounds, while Liang weighed a mere 125 pounds. Simple physics dictated that his horse should be faster given its lighter load, and indeed, Liang swiftly closed in on his prey, though not as quickly as he'd estimated.

Liang decided that the problem was his horse, which, like almost every human he'd encountered in the United States, seemed to be fat and lazy. Liang wished he'd had his own horse, a beautiful athletic Arabian that he'd purchased from a local horse rancher, instead of this oversize nag. The Arabian was too slight to comfortably carry most of the men working for B&B, but for a man of Liang's diminutive stature the horse was spot-on perfect.

Liang rode the chubby quarter horse at full gallop for nearly three miles before he started to get close enough to try another shot. He could tell that his horse was fading. Quarter horses were sprinters, not bred for stamina, and Liang knew if he kept up the pace for too long he'd kill his ride home. But if that was the case, he knew the quarter horse his opponent rode had to be at least as tired, and probably more so, given his additional burden.

Liang's quarry didn't appear to be doing much better than the horses they both rode. The lucky shot appeared to have done enough damage to inhibit the man's riding ability, but it didn't appear to be a kill shot. He had hoped to get closer for a better shot, but judging from his horse's condition he probably couldn't continue much longer. Liang stopped his horse to take a final shot, but before he had his rifle to his shoulder the big man had whirled his horse and fired off a shot of his own. The shot missed Liang, but it struck his horse in the neck. The animal fell to the ground, throwing Liang into some thorny sagebrush. By the time he'd extricated himself and gathered his weapon and the other gear he'd lost when he fell from the horse, the animal was dead and his opponent had disappeared.

HAD BOLAN BEEN prone to self-pity, he would have cursed the bad luck that had allowed his pursuer's wild shot to find its mark, which happened to be his left shoulder, but Bolan was a professional and he knew that this was all part of the game. He also knew that he could be thankful for his good luck, because the bullet had passed through muscle tissue without finding an artery or bone. But the soldier didn't expend a lot of energy thinking about luck, good or bad. Instead, he put his energy into making his own luck.

This time he'd need some help to make his luck good. Even though the bullet hadn't done any permanent damage, he was still bleeding profusely. He could feel himself getting weaker by the mile, but he continued at as fast a pace as he dared without killing his horse, trying to put as much distance as possible between himself and the Ag Con ranch. Once he was certain he'd shaken his pursuers, he dialed the number on the business card he'd been given the previous afternoon. He'd burned the card, but not before he'd memorized the number.

Kristen Kemp sounded glad to hear from him. "Are you all right?" she asked.

"I've been better," he said. He hated to bring a civilian into this mess, but Kemp was already involved, and judging from what he'd seen of Ag Con, she would probably be safer with him than by herself. Besides, he needed to have a bullet removed from his shoulder and have the wound sewn up, and Kemp had the skills to do the job. He didn't dare go to the local hospital for medical attention because Ag Con would most likely be watching for him there. And even if they weren't, the hospital would have to report his wound to the sheriff, which was as good as reporting his presence to Ag Con.

Bolan already knew that Ag Con somehow had its

hooks into the sheriff, which was the only possible explanation for the bogus incident report the sheriff filed after the Ag Con sniper had tried to kill him and Kemp the previous afternoon. The Executioner hadn't seen the report himself, but Kurtzman had obtained a copy of it the moment Buck entered it into the North Dakota State Bureau of Criminal Investigation computer system. The sheriff was dirty. How dirty, Bolan didn't know, but he did know the man couldn't be trusted.

"I've been shot," Bolan told Kemp.

"My God!" Kemp exclaimed. "Is it serious?"

"It's not good," he told her. "It could get serious in a hurry if I don't do something about it soon."

"Where are you?"

"I'm about a half-hour ride from where we parked the horse trailer yesterday. How soon can you be there?"

"It's about a forty-five-minute drive," she said. "I can be there in half an hour."

"Watch your back," Bolan warned. He tried to sound strong to keep from spooking Kemp, but after he put his phone away he realized he'd lost more blood than he'd thought. It took all the concentration he had to remain in the saddle and control his horse as it trotted through the rugged terrain. He checked his watch, more to give him something to focus on than to see the time, an attempt to keep from passing out.

Bolan used the last of his strength to negotiate the switchback trail that led down to the parking area where he was supposed to meet Kemp, feeling consciousness slipping away. The soldier summoned all the inner strength he could muster to dismount his horse and remove the saddle and bridle. The fewer clues he left for his pursuers, the better. When he was done, he gave the horse a weak slap on the rump and sent it scampering into the Badlands. The last thing he saw before he passed out on top of the saddle was a pair of headlights coming into the parking lot. He hoped to hell they belonged to Kemp's pickup.

"DID YOU STOP HIM?" Chen asked Liang over the radio.

"No, sir," Liang replied. "I wounded him, but he was able to kill the horse I was riding before I could get another shot at him. I am sorry, sir."

Chen knew that the colonel would stop at nothing in pursuit of prey—the man seemed to have no fear, even of death. If this intruder was able to make Liang break off the chase, especially after being wounded, then Chen knew they were up against a seasoned professional.

"Were you wounded?" he asked Liang.

"No, sir. My horse stopped the one bullet the man fired before he got away."

"Did you get a look at the man?"

"Not a good look, sir, but I believe it was the man who was with the veterinarian yesterday."

This news concerned Chen. Gordon Gould had sent him the information that the sheriff had collected on this man, Matt Cooper, and everything he'd seen worried him. There was nothing in the report that indicated that Cooper would present any problems, which in itself was the problem. The man was simply too clean. No messy divorces—no marriages for that matter—no disciplinary problems in the military, but also nothing outstanding. No criminal background, not even a parking ticket.

Everything pointed to a professional cleansing of this man's entire history. Such a thorough cleansing would require cooperation at the highest levels of government. It would also require resources far beyond the reach of any "security consultant," whatever that was. Clearly this

Cooper was well-connected, meaning he either worked for some governmental agency, or at the very least worked *with* one.

But which one? Not the CIA—of that Chen could be certain. Chen and his comrades were leaving nothing to chance; they were betting everything on the success of their plan. They had a man inside the CIA, and if the Agency had a resource on the ground in North Dakota, Chen would have known about it. Likewise Chen had eyes and ears inside the FBI and there was no activity from that quarter. The NSA was a tougher nut to crack, but as far as Chen knew, its operations began and ended with gathering information. The capacity to convert that information to genuine action seemed beyond them. And as far as Chen was concerned the Department of Homeland Security was pathetic beyond being even a joke, a bloated bureaucracy that was nothing more than a halfway house for utter incompetents owed political favors.

That eliminated every known source of this intrusion on their operations, but wasn't terribly helpful in deducing who actually did employ Cooper. Other than the obviously doctored background report that the sheriff had pulled, Chen knew only one thing about the large man—he was extremely dangerous. The man needed to be stopped.

"How far do you estimate Cooper has traveled since you last saw him?" Chen asked.

"Possibly two miles, no more than three."

Chen pondered his options. The helicopters were at the northeast unit of the ranch nearly one hundred miles away and could not be called back in time to help with the chase, and the terrain was too rough to use vehicles, even ATVs. The only way to pursue this intruder was on horseback. Chen needed to act fast if he was to have any chance of capturing Cooper.

"I'm sending out a patrol on horseback," he stated. "One of them will have your Arabian. I want you to meet up with them and get back on the trail of the intruder. Give me your GPS coordinates."

BOLAN WOKE UP to find himself lying on an operating table, but he wasn't in a hospital. A pair of bright green eyes peered at him from over a hospital face mask. Kristen Kemp sewed the last stitches into his shoulder. He watched her finish and then remove a needle from his left arm. She placed a cotton ball over the hole left by the needle and taped it down.

"You've lost a lot of blood," she told him. "By all rights you should still be sleeping."

"Are we in your clinic?" he asked. He looked around at the Spartan operation. He appeared to be in an operating room, lying on a stainless-steel table. Through an open door he saw a plain lobby bereft of plants, wall hangings, or other items that might provide comfort to a worried pet owner. This place was all business, like the people of the region themselves. It really was a large-animal clinic, a glorified metal barn designed to keep people's business tools—their horses and cattle—healthy. There didn't appear to be a lot of resources devoted to pampering pet owners.

"Why do you ask? You have a problem being treated by a veterinarian? Are you afraid I might get confused and neuter you?"

"In my line of work I consider having a bullet removed by a veterinarian luxury treatment," he said. "It beats doing it myself."

"That must be some line of work you have. I don't think I'm going to sign up for security-consulting duty any time soon."

Bolan sat up and tried to collect his thoughts. "How long was I out?" he asked.

"About an hour."

Bolan tried to focus on the logistics of what had just happened. By this point his pursuers may or may not have found his horse. "Did you bring my horse tack?" he asked.

"I figured it must have been important for you to take the time to remove it in your condition, so, yes, I made sure I grabbed it. You must be awfully fond of that saddle."

Bolan remained silent, contemplating the likelihood that they'd been followed. If the Ag Con men found his horse, they wouldn't be able to positively identify it as his, and without leaving the tack behind, they wouldn't have a starting point from which to begin their search. On the other hand, they knew that Bolan was somehow connected to Kemp, so they'd almost certainly come after her, meaning that they weren't safe here.

Kemp put her hands on Bolan's bare shoulders and tried to get him to lie back down. "You've lost a lot of blood," she repeated. "You should rest."

"We're not safe here," Bolan said.

"That's ridiculous," she said as she covered his wound with a sterile bandage. "Grassy Butte has 250 people, and I know every last one of them personally. No one's going to harm us here."

"Have you ever been shot at before yesterday?" he asked.

"No."

"Whatever you thought you knew about this place changed the moment that happened," he told her. "Grassy Butte suddenly became a whole lot less hospitable. Those 250 people you think you know? You can't trust any of them, not for the time being. Something big is going on here. I don't know what it is, but I do know that it's damned dangerous."

"Are you serious?" she asked. As Kemp leaned forward to apply another adhesive strip to his bandages, Bolan saw a shadow of a man holding what could only be a gun outlined in the window behind her. He reached out to grab the woman and flipped her over him. Before she landed on the hard-tiled floor, automatic gunfire tore through the corrugated steel that comprised the walls of the clinic. Bolan hurled himself down on top of her.

The bullets ripped through the metal walls, its insulation and inner plasterboard like they were paper, but the rounds didn't have enough energy to penetrate the stainless-steel operating table behind which Bolan and Kemp hunkered.

"Where are my weapons?" Bolan asked.

"I'm lying on them," Kemp replied. She rolled away to reveal most of Bolan's equipment—his handguns, extra magazines, binoculars and sat phone—along with an extremely bloody shirt with a large hole in the left shoulder.

Bolan pulled the Desert Eagle from its holster and chanced a peek around the edge of the operating table. He could see a streetlight, which was what cast the shadow that had alerted him to the shooter—likely just one of many, judging from the amount of lead flying through the clinic. From the angle of the light he estimated the location of the shooter, whose shadow he could still see in the window glass. He calculated where the man would be standing to cast a shadow at that angle, aimed and fired, punching several holes through the wall in that direction. The hot loads that John "Cowboy" Kissinger had loaded up for him back at Stony Man rammed through the wall at a tick over 1,500 feet per second and found their mark.

Bolan watched the shadow in the window drop to the ground, but the rounds kept pouring into the building.

"Is there another way out of here?" Bolan asked.

"Yeah, we can get out the back."

"That means they can get in the same way," Bolan said, "but I don't see many other options here." The door to the back was directly behind the operating table. Bolan noted that the shots were only coming at them from the front of the building. "I wonder why they aren't shooting at us from the back."

"They might be, but they'd have to penetrate about twenty feet of hay bales to reach us. We've got hay stored on that side of the building."

"Have you got any roof vents?"

"Of course," Kemp said. "We have to comply with building codes."

"Are they turbine vents?"

"No, only every other one is a turbine," Kemp said.

"That means we can get out through the others," Bolan said. "Follow me."

While they'd been discussing the building's specifics, Bolan had slipped into the shoulder rig that held his Beretta 93-R and extra magazines. He didn't bother with the destroyed, bloody shirt. He put the reloaded .44 Magnum handgun back in its holster, which he'd clipped onto his belt, and led the way into the back room with the Beretta.

Scoping out the rear room, which was really just a large barn, complete with pens occupied by various cows, sheep and horses, all of which were extremely distressed due to the gunfire, Bolan saw that the back door was still closed. "I wonder why they haven't come through the back door?" he asked.

"Probably because of Earl," Kemp said.

"Earl?"

"He's an especially foul-tempered Angus bull that we use for sperm," Kemp replied. "I think they're going to need something with a little more kick than a .223 to get past Earl."

Kemp and Bolan made their way to the stack of hay bales along the far wall. They scrambled to the top, then climbed into the metal rafters holding up the roof. The soldier punched out the first roof vent he found and they both climbed onto the roof, Bolan's feet clearing the vent milliseconds before the shooters burst through the front door.

Bolan looked over the peak of the roof and saw an SUV parked on the street a few feet away from the driveway that led into the clinic's parking lot. The vehicle appeared empty except for the driver, but it was hard to be certain because of the darkly tinted windows. He saw that the men in front of the building had entered through the front door, probably expecting to find perforated bodies. But the only person in the front of the building was the man Bolan had shot, and he wasn't moving. Two men stood guard at the rear of the building, just outside Earl's pen, waiting to see if anyone came out the back.

The drop to the ground was too far to risk jumping. A sprained or broken ankle would be a death sentence for both of them, but Bolan saw an option—a large manger filled with alfalfa for Earl to munch on. But first the soldier had to deal with the sentries, and he had to do it fast, because judging from the commotion in the building, the shooters had discovered that they hadn't succeeded in killing him and Kemp. Bolan aimed the sound-suppressed Beretta at the farthest sentry and drilled a round right between his eyes. The man's buddy saw him fall and looked up for the source of the coughing sound made by the

Beretta, but before he could raise his own gun, Bolan put a second round through the top of his head, dropping him like a stone. Then the Executioner stood up and fired three quick rounds through the SUV's open driver's window. It was dark inside the SUV cab, but Bolan saw the outline of spray issuing from the driver's head as the man slumped forward, setting off the SUV's horn.

"Now what?" Kemp asked.

"Now we jump." Bolan grabbed the woman around the waist and jumped down into Earl's manger. The falling bodies startled the bull and he lunged away. Before he comprehended the fact that he had visitors, both Bolan and Kemp were running for the corral. Earl gathered his wits and charged the pair, but they managed to grab the rail of the corral and hurl themselves out of the pen just before the bull crashed into its metal bars. That made Earl angrier, and he was about to charge the fence again when the back door opened and two gunmen came blundering into his pen. The gigantic black bull whirled and before the first man out knew what was happening, Earl ran him down and pummeled his body into the hay and manure. The man's partner froze, giving the bull an opening, which he put to good use, ramming the sentry against the steel building, snapping his spine.

Kemp and Bolan missed out on all the Earl-generated carnage because they'd jumped in a Yamaha Rhino ATV that Kemp and Bowman used for doing chores around the clinic property. The Rhino was a side-by-side ATV, meaning that rather than sitting astride it the occupants rode in bucket seats inside a Jeep-like cab. They'd already cleared the property and were heading into the Badlands by the time Earl had pulverized his second victim.

Bolan let Kemp drive the ATV. He had plenty of experience driving every type of off-road vehicle, but the vet knew how to operate this particular one and she knew the terrain.

"Where are we going?" he asked over the roar of the engine, which Kemp was running at full throttle.

"I know a safe place," she replied.

3

Killdeer Mountains, North Dakota

Chen's driver pulled off the highway and headed for the Ag Con facility on Gap Road. This facility operated on a much smaller scale than their main complex. It was really more of a family ranch than a large-scale cattle operation. Chen and his associates had selected it because of its isolation and inaccessibility—it was located so far back in the Badlands that they could land helicopters without alerting neighbors. It didn't afford much room for their research and development operations, but it was the perfect place to store a couple of prisoners.

Not that their presence hadn't raised suspicion among the locals. Chen and the other Chinese nationals working for Ag Con stuck out like the proverbial raisins in the oatmeal. That's why Ag Con relied on the mercenaries from Build & Berg Associates—they at least looked like the locals, and in fact even sounded like them. Many of the B&B mercs came from Eastern Europe, and western North Dakota had been settled by Ukrainians, Germans, Russians, Poles and Hungarians; Eastern European accents were still commonplace.

The locals were self-sufficient, and they valued their freedom. They didn't want to be bothered, and by the same token, they didn't bother anyone else. The locals didn't like confrontation and they kept to themselves. It was the perfect social climate for Ag Con's plans.

When Liang's troops lost the intruder's trail, Liang guessed that the man might try to contact the veterinarian. Since Cooper was wounded, Liang predicted he'd need medical attention, and where better to get that than in a clinic—even an animal clinic. He'd sent a six-man team to ambush the pair, but had lost contact with the men soon after they'd identified Cooper and Kemp inside the clinic. That could only mean that the ambush had failed. So he sent a second team to cleanse the scene of all evidence of Ag Con involvement.

The clinic was two miles north of town. Gunfire was a fairly normal occurrence in the area—target shooting was one of the few recreational activities the region offered—but a fusillade of automatic rifle fire at three o'clock in the morning would raise some eyebrows, even among the stoic locals. So after he'd sent the cleanup crew to the clinic, Chen called Gordon Gould and had him order Sheriff Buck to the scene. Buck was to report the shooting as an act of vandalism, but he was to report that there had not been any injuries. Chen wasn't as confident in Gould's ability to control the sheriff as was Gould himself. Forcing Buck to help dispose of bodies would certainly put Gould's claim of subservience on the sheriff's part to the test.

Chen was on his way to interrogate Pam Bowman, the second half of the pair of veterinarians. He needed to find Kemp and Cooper, and he needed to find them quickly.

He hadn't harmed his prisoners thus far simply because there had been no reason to do so, but on this visit he brought along a special toolkit. A civilized and fastidious man, Chen didn't look forward to the unhygienic act of torturing a woman, but expediency required him to do whatever was necessary to gain the information he needed.

Chen's driver turned off the road and stopped the vehicle. One of the two PLA regulars Chen had brought to assist him got out of the car, opened the gate and closed it again after the SUV had passed through the entrance. Chen would have preferred to install a modern electronic gate, but that would have attracted unwanted attention. Most people in the area used either a cattle grate dug into the road or else they used a primitive type of homemade gate. Though the gate may have been rustic, there was nothing antiquated about the electronic surveillance equipment that was hidden around the entire perimeter of the property. The main complex was too vast and sprawling to effectively monitor the perimeter using electronic methods, but that was not the case with the smaller ranch they'd purchased in the Killdeer Mountains. This facility was much more secure than the other operation.

They drove down the winding, seven-mile driveway that wound around the base of a massive butte and down into a deep ravine. The ravine opened up into a small triangular meadow surrounded on two sides by steep cliffs, and bordered on the third by a small creek. He couldn't see them, but he knew Liang's sharpshooters had every possible entrance and exit covered at all times.

His driver punched a button on a box clipped to his sun visor and an overhead door built into the side of an old barn rose open. When the driver had parked the SUV inside the barn, Chen got out and opened a creaky wooden door that apparently led into a storage area beneath the stairway that led up to the haymow. But instead of a storage area, he stepped into a metal lift that would take him down to the basement they had excavated deep beneath the barn. The basement contained the laboratory where much of Ag Con's real work took place. It was also where they held the veterinarian and the extension agent.

Chen opened the cell door and woke the occupants, who both appeared to have been asleep on the cots that Chen's men had provided. "I apologize for waking you," he said, "but I need some information from Ms. Bowman."

Grevoy started to rise from his cot, but Liang's soldiers restrained him. "Please secure Mr. Grevoy," Chen ordered. Liang's soldiers produced plastic zip ties and bound Grevoy's hands behind his back with brutal efficiency, then secured his feet to steel rings embedded in the concrete floor. The men then grabbed Pam Bowman and lifted her to her feet.

"Ms. Bowman, let me be perfectly clear. I need some information, and you will provide me with it. You will most likely resist, and I will be forced to extract it from you in a most uncivilized manner." Chen put on a lab coat, placed a mask over his face and put on a pair of latex gloves. One of Liang's soldiers handed a tool roll to Chen, who spread it out on the table and picked up what looked like a stainless-steel dental cleaning tool. "I assure you that I would prefer not to go to such lengths," Chen said from behind his mask, "but make no mistake, I will go to any length if you force my hand. Now please tell me, if Ms. Kemp had fled your clinic and was seeking sanctuary, where would she go?"

"I have no idea where she'd go," Bowman said.

"Of course, we both know you have some idea," Chen

said. "And of course you won't betray her unless you are forced to do so. So you are going to make me work to extract that information." He pulled out a pair of needle-nose pliers from the toolkit, along with a medical scalpel. "Since this might take a while, we might as well get started."

KEMP TORE across the Little Missouri National Grassland, the ATV's off-road suspension doing its best to cope with the rough terrain they covered at a much-too-high speed. Bolan wore lap and shoulder belts that kept him inside the vehicle, but he braced himself with both hands to prevent his bare head from banging against the built-in roll cage. He had no idea where she was going. Their destination could be anywhere in the vast grassland, the largest national grassland in the country, covering over 1.6 million acres.

They started to ride down into the Badlands, the bentonite buttes rising up alongside them, and Bolan thought they would soon have to abandon the vehicle, but then they came across an oil-field road that wound along the bottom of a gully. "Road" was a bit of a stretch for the trails the oil company built throughout the Badlands to allow their service crews to reach their oil pumping rigs. There were thousands of miles of these oil-field roads.

Kemp cranked the wheel of the ATV, barely slowing, all four wheels kicking up rooster tails of dust and earth. Once the vehicle had settled enough for him to free his hands, Bolan pulled out the sat phone and punched in the number for the secure line to Stony Man Farm.

"Striker!" Barbara Price answered, using Bolan's Stony Man code name. "You're still alive!"

"You had doubts?"

"The last time the Bear heard from you, your conversation ended with automatic weapon fire that practically deafened him," Price said. "Are you okay?"

"I'm fine."

"Glad to hear it," she said. Price was a consummate professional and wouldn't let her personal feelings come into play during a mission, but Bolan could hear a hint of relief in her voice. Bolan and the beautiful blonde who was mission controller at Stony Man Farm had been occasional lovers for years.

"Any new information on Ag Con?" Bolan asked.

"Nothing on Ag Con, but we've dug up a bunch of information about their security firm."

"Who are they using?"

"Build & Berg Associates."

"Why would they need a bunch of cutthroat mercenaries to guard a cattle ranch?" Bolan asked.

"Good question," Price replied. "They must have some mean coyotes out there."

"I think they've got more than that," Bolan said. "I think they've bolstered the B&B mercs with some PLA regulars. I'm pretty sure the man who shot me wasn't with B&B."

"You've been shot?"

"It's nothing," Bolan said. "I'm all right. I'm in good hands." He looked over at Kemp, who was listening to his end of the conversation as best she could over the engine noise.

"How many B&B goons do they have on staff?" he asked.

"According to their records, they've got 225, which makes no sense at all."

"None of this makes sense," Bolan said. "Why would a corporate cattle operation want to kidnap a veterinarian and a county extension agent in the first place?"

"You've confirmed that Ag Con has kidnapped Bowman and Grevoy?"

"Affirmative," Bolan said. "I saw them being taken from the facility in a helicopter. Something big is going on here."

"You're right, Striker. We'll keep looking into it on this end."

"You could start by seeing if you can find out where the helicopters took Bowman and Grevoy."

"We'll do our best. Normally we'd be able to track them with satellites, but there aren't a lot of eyes in the sky pointed at western North Dakota. We'll see if we can find anything. In the meantime, you try not to get shot again."

"I'll do my best."

"Girlfriend?" Kemp asked once he'd hung up.

"She's a woman, and she's a friend. She's also a colleague."

"Is she your boss at your security consulting company?"

"A contact," he replied. "Where are we going?"

"Someplace safe," she said. She turned off the road and followed a barely discernable trail through a pasture until they came to a barbed-wire fence. "Open the gate," Kemp ordered. Bolan did as he was told, closing the gate behind him and getting back into the ATV. He estimated they'd traveled about four miles when they came upon a cottage—a shack, really—with walls made of small-diameter stones. The structure looked as if it had been here for well over a century, but the shiny steel that covered the roof spoke of recent renovation.

"We're here," Kemp said.

"Where's 'here'?"

Kemp got out of the ATV. Bolan followed her as she went behind the shack and unlocked the doors to a small wood-framed structure that stood about two feet high. Inside the structure sat a powerful generator, along with a pressure pump, indicating that the structure stood atop a water well.

"'Here' is the hunting shack that Pam and I built when we were still together. Well, we didn't really 'build' it, since this building has been here since before North Dakota was a state. I guess I should say that we remodeled it." She primed the generator several times, pulled the choke, and the quiet engine started up. She unlatched the shingled roof of the small structure, which was on hinges, and propped it up with a two-by-four that had been attached to the underside of the roof, creating a vent through which the generator's exhaust gases could escape while still protecting the generator from the elements.

"Let's go inside and get cleaned up," she said.

The interior of the cabin was simple but comfortable, a single room with a small closet-size area partitioned off for the toilet. The shower, consisting of a see-through plastic curtain surrounding a drain, with a hose running from a faucet to a showerhead suspended from the rafters, stood in one corner. "Since it was just the two of us using the place we didn't see the need for privacy," Kemp said. "I hope you don't mind."

Bolan made himself comfortable, and Kemp scrubbed her hands in the sink. "Let me check your wound," she said. "You shouldn't have been so active so soon."

"I didn't see a lot of options," Bolan said.

"You seem to attract trouble."

"It's an occupational hazard."

Kemp looked at Bolan and started to make another comment about the nature of being a security consultant, but shut her mouth before any sound came out and just shook her head. She removed the bandage.

"The stitches have held," she said, "but you're still bleeding." She cleaned the wound, applied some antiseptic cream, then unlocked a metal cabinet on one wall and took out a can of heavy-duty wound sealant.

"You're lucky I'm equipped for dealing with large animals that are too dumb to lie around and heal up after they've been injured," she said, spraying the sealant over the stitches that closed up the bullet's entrance wound over the soldier's shoulder. "Normally this is where I'd put some bitter-tasting spray on the wound to keep you from licking it, but I'm going to give you the benefit of the doubt."

"I promise not to lick my wounds," Bolan assured her.

"This doesn't look the first time you've taken a bullet," Kemp said, looking up and down the big man's bare torso. "It doesn't look like the second, or even the tenth. Do you even know how many times you've been shot?"

"I've lost track," the soldier said truthfully.

She started to respond, but again thought better of it and just shook her head. She put a fresh bandage over the wound, then peeled something that looked like adhesive-backed plastic off a roll she pulled from her medicine cabinet and placed it over the bandage.

"You can shower first," she told him. "If you want some privacy I'll wait outside."

"I'm not shy," Bolan said, removing his clothes and stepping into the shower. When he finished, she was waiting for him with a clean towel.

"Do you want me to step out while you shower?" he asked her.

"Sure. Thanks."

Ten minutes later, she called Bolan back inside. Fully clothed, they shared the one bed and curled up to get some sleep.

"OH JEEZ!" Jim Buck moaned.

"Shut your fucking mouth, Jim!" Gordon Gould ordered, but the sheriff kept muttering "Oh jeez! Oh jeez!" over and over as if the phrase was his new mantra. Gould was going to have to keep an eye on Buck. The carnage they'd discovered at the veterinarian clinic seemed to have unhinged the man. Gould pulled his nephew Jason into an examination room off the main lobby.

"Watch Jim," he told the younger Gould. "He looks about one fart away from losing his shit."

Liang joined the pair in the examination room. The Chinese seemed to share Gould's doubts about the sheriff's state of mind. "Are you absolutely certain you have Mr. Buck under control?" Liang asked.

"One hundred percent," Gould said, trying to sound more confident than he felt.

"I hope so, because the sheriff appears to be weeping. It's making my men nervous." Liang's men had removed the body from the front of the building, as well as the two men who had been shot outside the bull's pen out back. They'd also driven away the SUV, complete with its deceased driver. They had, however, left the bodies of the two men killed by the bull, which they'd barely managed to herd back into its pen; it had been eating hay inside the barn area of the clinic when Liang's men arrived. "Does the sheriff understand what he is to put in the report?"

"I think I'm going to have to help him some with that," Gould said.

"And *you* know what to put in the report?" Liang asked.

"I think so. Those two out back got fired from Ag Con today because they didn't like foreigners and lesbians."

"Because they displayed hostility toward minorities

and other protected groups and acted inappropriately," Liang corrected. "Such behavior is not allowed per Ag Con's employee handbook."

"Right," Gould said, "because they were inappropriate. Anyway, they got fired and decided to take out their frustration by vandalizing the lesbians' clinic, and ended up getting the shit stomped out of them by the clinic's prize Angus bull."

"I suppose that will have to suffice. Are you certain you can convince Sheriff Buck to fill out the report as you described?"

"That fat son of a bitch will fill it out any way I tell him," Gould said.

"If you have such omnipotent control over the man," Liang said, "perhaps you could convince him to leave. His whimpering is making my men nervous and hampering our cleanup operation."

"Jason, take Sheriff Buck to my house. Stay with him until I show up, and make damned sure he doesn't call anyone or fill out any incident reports until I get there." Gould felt embarrassed for Buck. He found the man's blubbering as annoying as any of the Ag Con men did, but he could see why Buck was upset. They had encountered one hell of a sight when they'd arrived at the animal hospital. The man in the SUV had had half his head blown off, and bloody chunks of bone and brain had sprayed the interior of the cab. Gould didn't envy the poor bastards who'd had to drive that vehicle to wherever Ag Con dumped it. The guy out front looked like he'd been shot in the gut with a cannon. He appeared to have been trying to stuff his intestines back in his body cavity when he died. And those two out back who had been stomped by the bull—Gould had never seen anything like that.

After Jason took the sheriff home, Gould watched the

Ag Con crew deal with the mess. They seemed to have some experience cleaning up human guts and brains. Gould felt cold fear wash over him as he watched the passionless men work. What have I gotten myself into? he wondered, but it was too late to back out. Ag Con had paid him more for what had so far amounted to just a few hours of work than he would ever make from his cattle operations and his salary as president of the North Dakota Cattle Raisers' Association combined—but he was starting to wonder if it had been worth it.

He was used to doing business with slimeballs and sleazebags of every stripe. That was par for the course when dealing with the North Dakota state legislature. And he'd resorted to extreme measures to protect the association and in particular to protect his presidency. Gould was no Boy Scout. He'd killed men in Vietnam, and had arranged for a couple of obstinate ranchers who had gotten in his way to meet the same fate. But he was starting to worry that this time he had made a deal with the devil himself.

Liang's cell phone rang, and the man stepped outside to take the call. When he came back in, he walked over to the corner in which Gould was brooding.

"Mr. Gould," he said, "you are to go get Sheriff Buck and bring him to your office. Please make certain that he knows exactly what he is to say and write before he goes to the police station to prepare his report. And please, stick to the script that I have prepared for you." Liang handed Gould some notes scrawled by hand on a yellow legal tablet. "You are to burn these papers after you have coached Sheriff Buck. No improvisation, please."

These people would say "please" and "thank you" when they killed you, Gould thought.

"Go immediately, please," Liang said.

BOLAN WOKE UP to the sound of distant engines approaching. Kemp had fallen asleep curled up against him, and he had his arm across her waist. "Wake up," he whispered. "We've got company."

Bolan had rolled out of bed and had boots on before she was even completely awake. The sound of engines was still off in the distance. Their drone carried for miles through the stillness of the night, but they were approaching fast.

"You have a shirt I could wear?" he asked.

"You might be in luck," Kemp said, buttoning her jeans. "Try this." She pulled a large flannel shirt from a steel bureau beside the bed. "I use this as a nightgown. It just might fit you." It did.

"What have you got for weapons?" Bolan asked.

Kemp produced a key and opened a locked steel cabinet to reveal a variety of rifles and one handgun, a Ruger Super Blackhawk revolver chambered for .44 Magnum rounds. Bolan selected a Browning BAR deer rifle chambered for the .308 Winchester round, along with several loaded 4-round magazines that sat on a shelf inside the cabinet. "Extra ammo?" he asked.

Kemp pulled four 20-round boxes of 165-grain Remington Core-Lokt rounds. She then selected a Savage bolt-action rifle that was chambered for the .30-06 Springfield round and put the Ruger in a Western-style holster she'd strapped around her waist.

Kemp tossed the soldier the .308 ammo along with several boxes of Core-Lokt rounds in a camouflage backpack and a couple of 50-round boxes of Remington Desert Eagle .44 Magnum ammo. Again, it was nothing fancy compared to the custom-loaded ammunition Bolan was used to shooting, but effective nonetheless.

"Let's get out of here," he said. "Is there a way out the back?"

"There's a vent window in the toilet area. I'll fit through it. You might, too," she said, looking at the soldier's broad shoulders, "but just barely."

"Then let's get out of here," Bolan said. He squeezed through the window and was helping Kemp through when a rifle shot shattered the window that faced out the front of the cabin. The first shot was followed by a barrage of rifle fire. If they had been shooting at a wood-frame building, the bullets would have passed through the walls and turned the interior of the cabin into a killing box, but the .223 bullets from the attackers' Chinese rifles just ricocheted off the stone walls.

The sun was only just coming up so there still wasn't much light, but Bolan's well-trained eyes caught movement to his right. He let go of Kemp, who tumbled through the window to the ground, and brought his rifle to his shoulder. The Nikon Monarch UCC scope on his gun featured a special light-gathering coating and when he looked through its lens he could clearly see the figure of a man creeping through the sagebrush, trying to get around to the back of the cabin. Bolan centered the crosshairs of the scope on the man's chest and squeezed the trigger. The recoil of the rifle pushed the scope up, but when Bolan brought it back down, he saw the man sprawled out on the ground facedown, a crimson pool of blood spreading out around his torso.

Kemp had regained her composure and grabbed her gun. "This way," she said, and broke into a run. Bolan followed her as she ran to a path that led down a steep cliff to a dry creek bed.

"We can circle around behind them and get to a better shooting position," she said. "We have a blind set up for hunting deer that looks right down on the approach to the cabin." The speed with which Kemp moved and her sure-footedness impressed Bolan.

The pair ran up a switchback trail that ended on a small plateau atop a butte that overlooked the cabin. Bolan crawled to the edge of the cliff and surveyed the scene through the scope of his Browning rifle. At least two dozen men were firing at the front of the cabin and Bolan could hear shots coming from behind the structure. So far no one seemed to have realized that their quarry had escaped. Kemp had taken up a shooting position beside him and had her scope on a potential target.

"What should we do?" she asked him. "There are at least twenty-five men down there. Should we take them on or should we get the hell out of here?"

"Where would we go?" Bolan asked.

"That's a bit of a problem," Kemp replied. "The only way out of here is the way we came in. We're in some seriously rugged country. When they realize we're not inside the cabin, they're going to be coming out on our heels. This is as good a position as we're going to find to take them on."

"Then let's do it." Bolan said, squeezing the trigger, taking out one of the Build & Berg mercenaries. Kemp did the same, with the same result. The Executioner took out four more of the men below, and Kemp dropped another two before the mercenaries realized they were under attack from the rear. They dropped another three before the B&B men below were able to get enough of a fix on their position and start returning fire.

When the bullets from below started getting too close for comfort, Kemp said, "Follow me." She ran in a crouch toward a crevice in the side of the butte. She slid down the crevice on her rear until it ended about halfway down the side of the butte. She ran along a trail that led to a juniper tree with a metal deer stand resting against it.

"You get up there—you'll have good sight lines to the cabin." It was a good hide for the soldier because the sun rising behind the butte would make it hard for the men to pinpoint his muzzle-flashes through the brush. With each passing minute Bolan became more impressed with Kemp.

"I'll go to the base of the butte and get the stragglers you miss," the woman said. Bolan scrambled up the deer stand. When he looked through his scope, he saw the remaining B&B mercenaries creeping toward the butte. He counted eight men left standing. That left at least five unaccounted for, meaning they were probably circling around to attack them from behind. He set his crosshairs on the nearest man, who was within two hundred yards of the base of the butte, and squeezed the trigger. His scope rose toward the sky, but he acquired another target almost before the action of the rifle had finished cycling another round into the chamber and dropped another man. He sighted in on a third man, but before he could squeeze the trigger he heard a shot from below and the man fell to the ground with half his head missing.

Bolan sighted in on another target and squeezed the trigger, hearing Kemp do the same. He tried to find another target, but the remaining three men had taken cover. He scoped out the area and saw the top of a head poking out from behind some sagebrush. There wasn't much besides sage to hide behind on the killing fields below, but it might just as well have been nothing. Bolan set his crosshairs just below the tuft of hair and squeezed the trigger. He was rewarded with the sight of the scalp flying skyward.

The soldier reloaded his rifle, slamming the last of

his loaded magazines in place of the depleted one. Kemp had all of their ammo in her backpack. Not counting the men who were probably circling around the butte to attack them from behind, there were only two shooters left. Their opponents didn't seem to be the best-organized group Bolan had ever encountered, and they didn't seem used to encountering resistance, but he knew better than to assume they were completely stupid. He scanned the area looking for the remaining two shooters. He didn't see anyone, but then he heard a shot and saw a blood smear appear along a shallow ridge that afforded one of the few hiding spots in the plain below the butte.

Bolan heard movement above him. He had no idea how many men were following them, but he knew there were at least five, and he had only four rounds left in his BAR. He slung the rifle and unholstered his Beretta. The sound suppressor was still screwed to the barrel, which suited the soldier's purpose. He crawled down from the deer stand and started climbing up the side of the butte as silently as possible. He could hear the men above making their way down the switchback trail that led to the stand. Using that route meant that it would take the men much longer to reach the deer stand than it had taken Bolan and Kemp when they slid down through the crevice. As they made their way down the trail, Bolan crept up the side of the butte. At one point the men passed on the path only a few feet above his location. He counted eight pairs of boots treading on the path above him.

After the last pair of boots passed by, Bolan counted to ten, then pulled himself up onto the path. All but two of the men had disappeared around the next switchback in the trail. The two remaining turned to see what had caused the noise on the trail behind them, but before they could make out the source, Bolan's Beretta coughed twice, putting a round into each man's head. A third man appeared on the trail and met the same fate as his comrades.

Bolan heard a shot from below, the loud boom of a high-powered rifle. It definitely came from Kemp's .30-06 and not one of the .223s carried by the B&B goons. He hoped her shot had been on target, but he didn't have a lot of time to think about that because the men below him had opened up. Their rounds flew over his head; the shooters were just taking wild potshots. To get to a position that would allow them to get a good shot at the soldier, they'd have to put themselves in his line of fire, so the mercenaries were just spraying and praying. The men couldn't get a good shot at Bolan, but at the same time he couldn't get a good shot at them.

The soldier was considering his options when he heard the booming report of Kemp's bolt-action Savage. From the sound, she had to have been coming up the path. The men below him returned fire, and Bolan once again heard the roar of Kemp's .30-06. He watched the trail below him and saw three men moving backward into his field of fire, their attention focused on Kemp's attack from below. It was a fatal mistake. Bolan switched his Beretta to 3-round-burst mode and emptied his 20-round magazine into the trio. He heard Kemp's rifle fire two more rounds, both of which hit the dead bodies lying on the trail below Bolan. After that, the silence that normally enveloped the Badlands resumed.

Bolan looked at the carnage below him through his rifle scope. No one down there appeared to be alive. After a few moments he heard Kemp shout, "Are you all right?"

"Yeah. You?"

"I guess," she said. "I think we've got them all."

"Okay. I'm coming down." Bolan jogged down the trail and rounded the switchback to see the barrel of Kemp's gun pointed up at him. When she saw him she lowered the barrel.

"Are you really all right?" he asked.

"No. I mean, yeah, I'm not hurt. But damn…" Bolan moved down the path until he was beside her. "I'm a doctor," she said. "My job is to save lives, not take them."

Bolan didn't say anything. People responded to the stress of combat in different ways. Kemp was one of the toughest people he'd ever met, but no one who'd ever taken a life in combat escaped without some psychological scarring. He'd have to keep an eye on her to make sure she didn't crack under the pressure.

4

Watford City, North Dakota

"Have a drink, you damned old fool," Jason Gould ordered Sheriff Jim Buck.

"I ain't drinking with you, you little cocksucker," Buck said.

"Suit yourself," Jason said. "Since it's just me drinking, I suppose I can break out Uncle Gordie's good stuff." Jason felt along beneath the counter lip of the liquor cabinet and produced a key. He unlocked the cupboard over the sink, pulled out a bottle of Johnnie Walker Blue Label whisky, and poured the liquor into an oversize tumbler he'd filled with ice. He sat down on a couch, drinking from the tumbler in big gulps, barely tasting the expensive whiskey.

"Might as well make yourself comfortable," Jason told Buck. "We ain't going nowhere until Gordie gets here." Jason produced a small glass pipe filled with yellowish chunks and a small butane torch. "I don't suppose you want to get high?"

"Hell, no," Buck said, "and you ain't going to be smoking that shit, either."

"Hell I ain't," Jason said, lighting the torch and holding it to the pipe. After holding the torch to the glass for a few moments, smoke started to rise from the chunks inside it, giving off a horrible caustic smell. Jason inhaled the smoke and held it in his lungs for several seconds, until he coughed it up. He closed his eyes, and when he opened them a few seconds later, he looked even crazier than usual. "What the hell you going to do to stop me? You can't stop me from doing nothing. You can't even stop me from getting *special favors* from your old lady."

Buck lunged at the young man, but Jason produced a Springfield XD pistol from a holster that he'd clipped inside the waistband of his jeans. "You really think that's a good idea, Jim? You really want both you and Linda going to prison? Who's going to take care of your kids? You've seen what happens to kids in foster homes. You really want that to happen to your kids? Now sit your fat ass down and wait for my uncle to get here."

Buck sat down in a recliner and watched the young tweaker scratching at the scabby skin on his neck. He still held the gun in his hand and he seemed to intend to aim it at Buck, but his hand shook so hard that it was pointing all over the room. Jason seemed so high that Buck wasn't sure he knew exactly what was going on. Not that it mattered; the Goulds had Buck by his balls.

Jason fidgeted with the gun for a few moments, then returned it to the inside-the-waistband holster and returned to drinking his whisky. Buck figured he might as well have a drink himself and went to the liquor cabinet. When he picked up the bottle of Johnnie Walker, Jason said, "What the fuck are you doing?"

"Getting a drink."

"Not from that bottle. No fucking way. You can drink from the Jameson." Buck put the bottle down and picked up the bottle of Jameson that sat on the counter. He didn't even bother with a glass; he took the whole bottle and sat back down in the recliner.

"Goddamn, look at you," Jason said. "You are one fat fuck. What the hell is a woman like Linda doing with a man like you?"

"And you're a damned drug addict," Buck said. "What's she doing with either of us?"

"She doesn't seem too particular about who she's with," Jason said. "She'll go out with just about anyone who's got a twenty-dollar bill when she's having a bad night at the casino." If the younger Gould hadn't been high on meth, he'd have seen that he was pushing Buck to the man's breaking point, but he wasn't known for his good judgment even during the rare moments when he was sober. All Jason saw was a fat man drinking whiskey straight from the bottle so he kept right on talking.

"She's had more pricks in her than a porcupine."

Buck kept listening and drinking, until he was no longer listening and only drinking. He kept drinking until he lifted the bottle and nothing more came out. He looked at the scrawny, scab-faced tweaker sitting across from him and saw his mouth moving, but he heard nothing except the rushing of blood in his head.

He'd known that Linda had a gambling problem, but he never knew the extent. He hadn't known she was stealing drugs from the evidence room, and he had no idea that she'd been unfaithful to him. He knew she stayed out late at the casino, but he hadn't wanted to think about that too much. He preferred to believe her when she told him she'd had a little too much to drink and had stayed with a friend.

He supposed he really had known, maybe not the full magnitude of what was going on, but at least that something wasn't right. He just preferred to believe Linda because he'd been too afraid to confront his deepest suspicions. He was afraid he didn't have the strength to handle it, and he was probably right. Now that he knew the truth, it was more than he could take.

He turned the bottle of whiskey upside down and a few drops dribbled on the floor. He dropped the bottle, walked over to the liquor cabinet and picked up the bottle of Johnnie Walker.

"I told you not to drink from that bottle," Jason said. "Put it down."

Buck just looked at him and took a pull from the bottle. The young man stood up and walked toward the sheriff, who responded with another drink of whisky.

"I said put it down, you fat fuck."

Buck put the bottle down and Jason relaxed. He turned to go sit down, but before he'd reached the couch, Buck had drawn his sidearm. "Jason," he said.

"What?" The young man turned and when he saw the gun pointed at his face his mouth went slack and his jaw dropped to his chest. Before Jason could utter a sound, Buck squeezed the trigger and a crater appeared in the center of the man's forehead. When Jason fell to the floor, the sheriff admired the symmetrical pattern of sprayed brains and blood on the wall behind where Jason had been standing. He took the bottle and sat back down in the recliner. He drank the remaining whisky in the bottle, then put his service pistol in his own mouth and pulled the trigger.

Trotters, North Dakota

JOZEF KOLODZIEJ, the man in charge of the Build &
Berg mercenaries hired by Ag Con, winced as the Chinese commander chewed him out in Kolodziej's native
Polish. Liang spoke perfect Polish, with very little hint of
an accent. Liang's command of the language was strong
enough to call Kolodziej a *matkojebca,* which, roughly
translated, suggested Kolodziej had carnal knowledge of
his own mother.

Under normal circumstances Kolodziej would not have
let anyone abuse him in that manner, but in this case there
was nothing he could say in his own defense. He had lost
over twenty-five percent of his men, apparently at the
hands of a single man and a veterinarian. Twice he had
sent what should have been overwhelming forces after the
pair, and twice those entire forces had been wiped out.
Liang had every reason to doubt the man's competence,
so Kolodziej suffered the verbal assault from the man in
silence.

"We are spending a great deal of money to procure
protection from Build & Berg," Liang said. "And we
expect performance commensurate with your fees." The
colonel stopped short of threatening Kolodziej or B&B.
Both men knew that such threats would be empty, since
Ag Con's master plan was too far along to make whole-
sale changes at this point. Kolodziej didn't know what
that plan was, but he hadn't been assigned to find out.
His job was simply to provide the brute force that Ag Con
needed.

Liang was not going to fire B&B, but that didn't mean
Kolodziej would escape unscathed once his superiors at
B&B learned of his men's multiple failures in capturing
the tall American whom Ag Con had deemed a threat.

Build & Berg had rewarded him handsomely for services rendered in the past, but he'd seen them deal with failure on the harshest possible terms. A B&B severance package didn't consist of several months' worth of wages—it consisted of the disappearance of the person being severed.

When Liang finished berating Kolodziej, the man retired to his office to try to find some information on his mysterious American opponent. He had contacts in various European intelligence organizations, and it was time to call in some favors. His life just might depend on it.

KEMP PILOTED the Rhino down an ATV trail used by local ranchers to monitor their herds. Four-wheeled all-terrain vehicles had almost entirely replaced horses as the mount of choice for ranchers, though the ranchers who had grazing land mixed in among the roughest terrain still had to rely on horses to reach some of their herds. Kemp once again demonstrated her tactical acumen by using these existing trails; there was no way that the B&B mercs would be able to distinguish their tire tracks from the dozens of other identical tracks pounded into the path.

Kemp had loaded the utility box on the back of the ATV with camping gear, food, water and ammo. He trusted her to find a safe hiding place in the vast grasslands, and they had enough supplies to hide out practically indefinitely. But hiding wasn't going to rescue Grevoy or Bowman, and it wasn't going to help Bolan find out what Ag Con was up to. He'd need to plan some sort of an offense, but so far he'd been too busy playing defense to develop one.

When Kemp turned onto a trail that led into a narrow pasture bordered on two sides by steep cliffs, Bolan estimated that they'd been on the trail for approximately seven miles, given the Rhino's top speed of forty-five miles per hour and the nine minutes that had passed. At the far end of the pasture Kemp turned into a wooded draw and drove the ATV deep into the brush.

"Help me cover this thing up," she said and began gathering juniper branches and sage, using it to camouflage the Rhino. "I don't know what in the hell is going on here, but these people seem adamant about finding us."

"How do you think they found your cabin?" Bolan asked. "Who else knew about it besides you and Bowman?"

"No one," Kemp said. "We never mentioned the place to anyone."

"Did Bowman ever bring anyone else out here?"

"No. She's seeing some chick from Denver. She's never had her out here, though. I've never met her. I don't even know her name. There's no way she knows about the cabin and probably doesn't even know Pam's been abducted."

"So the only way they could have found out about the cabin is if Ms. Bowman told them."

"I can't believe Pam would ever do anything to hurt me," Kemp said.

Bolan knew that her captors could extract whatever information they needed regardless of how stoic Bowman had been. He suspected that Kemp was well aware of this, too, but just didn't want to think about her former lover being tortured.

When they were finished covering the ATV, they set up a tent and covered that with brush and branches, too. They'd just finished and were putting their supplies inside the tent when Bolan's sat phone vibrated.

"Striker, I'm glad to hear you're still alive," Kurtzman said. "I have something for you about Roger's samples. The prions he found were nasty little buggers. We've never seen anything like them. They can cause mad cow disease in a matter of weeks, not years. He was wrong about their being mutations, though. The samples he supplied show signs of being genetically manipulated."

"Do you know who did the manipulating?" Bolan asked.

"No, but I can guess."

"So can I," Bolan said. "Our Chinese friends bankrolling Ag Con. Have you found out anything more on them?"

"Nothing certain, but I think the process of elimination indicates that they're our culprits. And if their intent is to poison the country's food supply, these prions will do the job. If these things get into cattle headed to the slaughter-houses, we'll start seeing Creutzfeldt-Jakob Disease hitting thousands, maybe millions of people within a month or two."

"How would they get it into the food supply?"

"Ag Con is the biggest distributor of cattle feed in the Midwest," Kurtzman said. "They supply most of the large-scale industrial feedlots in the country. It wouldn't be difficult for them to spike the feed with prions."

"Are you certain they haven't already done it?" Bolan asked.

"No, but so far we haven't seen any outbreaks of Creutzfeldt-Jakob. Our research indicates that anyone consuming meat infected with these prions would start to show symptoms within two to four weeks."

"Are you checking the slaughterhouses for infected cattle?"

"We've got teams of scientists posing as FDA inspectors hitting the slaughterhouses as we speak, but that's like hauling water in a wicker basket."

"Have you got contingency plans in place in case this stuff hits the food supply?"

"Hal's been keeping the President briefed about the

situation, but he doesn't want to put a ban on beef unless he absolutely has to." Kurtzman was referring to Hal Brognola. "The President thinks that banning the sale of beef would send the rural economy into a tailspin from which it might never recover. With all of the other economic challenges the country's currently facing, that would be enough to send our entire economic system into total collapse."

"He's probably right, but if this stuff gets out, he might have to choose between total economic collapse and the deaths of millions of people."

"Either way," Kurtzman said, "Ag Con wins. Unless you can shut down Ag Con before they get the chance to spike the feed supply with the prions."

"That's the third option, but that's not looking like a simple job at the moment. I could use a little help. What else have you got for me?" Bolan asked.

"The head of the Build & Berg operations at Ag Con is a man named Jozef Kolodziej."

"The name doesn't ring a bell. I've encountered him before?"

"No, but you have had a run-in with one of his associates—Florjan Adamczyk."

"Anything else?" Bolan asked.

"Yeah, we think we may have located a likely destination for the helicopters you saw taking Roger and Bowman away from the Ag Con compound. We didn't find out anything from satellite surveillance, but we checked the records and Ag Con owns a second facility in the Killdeer Mountains. I'll text you the GPS coordinates."

While he spoke with Kurtzman, Bolan watched Kemp remove her shirt, pour some water in a basin and begin washing off the dust and grime from the trail. When he finished talking to Kurtzman, he went over and joined her.

"What do we do now?" she asked.

"We wait for dark," he said.

"Then what?" she asked.

"How far are we from the Killdeer Mountains?"

"About twenty miles, if we take the highway, but that probably wouldn't be the smartest route for us to take."

"Probably not," the soldier said. "Are there back routes?"

"I can get us there without taking any improved roads," Kemp said, "but it will take us at least two hours. When do you want to go?"

"Not until after dark," Bolan said.

CHEN WAS GROWING tired of chasing Cooper around the state. The hunt was depleting his resources. Worse yet, it was distracting him from the matter at hand. The team developing the prions felt it was nearly ready to put its plans into motion, but with this latest intrusion Chen worried the team may be running out of time and would have to speed up its schedule. That would not be a simple task. The timing of the product had to be perfected. If the prions caused the cattle to become sick before they reached the slaughterhouse, the illness would be detected and the infected meat wouldn't reach the food supply. And if the infection didn't take hold quickly enough, the meat wouldn't be infected when it reached the food supply.

Chen knew that even if they didn't time everything just right, simply the threat of a contaminated food supply may be enough to collapse the economy of the Midwest, and in turn bring down the entire country's economy. The entire corrupt capitalistic system was so fragile that if the U.S. economy went down, the economy of the entire world would implode with it. Not since the decadent final days of ancient Rome had one empire spread its tentacles over such a large percentage of the world's population. Seamstresses in Pakistan, laborers in Vietnam, even prisoners in Chinese prisons depended on the U.S. economy to provide for their well-being. These fools needed to see the inherent weakness of the basket in which they'd placed all of their eggs.

The world would see the inequalities and corruption inherent in capitalism when Chen and his comrades brought the U.S. economy to its knees. This extreme action shouldn't have been necessary. The U.S. economy would have imploded years ago if China hadn't been propping up the U.S. government for much of the past decade with low-interest loans.

Chen cursed the misguided leaders of his country. It was bad enough that they provided the funding that allowed the decadent Americans to continue to prosper, but even more than that Chen resented the fact that China had increasingly adopted the corrupt capitalistic economic philosophy of the Americans. He felt fortunate to have hooked up with like-minded individuals who were in a position to reverse the direction his country had taken. Once their plan succeeded, the people of the world would turn their back on capitalism and once again embrace socialism.

Chen appreciated the irony of the fact that he and his comrades were using capitalism—the very tool they despised—to destroy the American economy. It was their success in the business world that provided the funding to purchase Agricultural Conglomerates. The fact that the Americans had allowed a foreign country to purchase a U.S. corporation that controlled a vast portion of the U.S. food supply provided testimony to the greed inherent in a capitalistic system. The Americans placed more value on the dollars the Chinese provided than on keeping the country's citizens safe and its society secure. At least China would never allow the Americans to purchase a Chinese corporation that controlled the single largest percentage of the Chinese food supply.

There had been some uproar about a group of Chinese investors purchasing Ag Con, but the naysayers had been written off as isolationists who failed to grasp the global nature of the U.S. economy. The business community approved of the sale, and the U.S. Congress had allowed the sale without any restrictions whatsoever.

Chen and his colleagues had already been working to develop a fast-acting prion even before the sale was approved. Once they had control of Ag Con, all the pieces had been put in place, and it was only a matter of perfecting the prion—something his team felt it had very nearly accomplished. The team had been in the process of testing on an isolated herd when the extension agent and the veterinarian had blundered onto the scene.

That was the first time something had not gone completely according to their plans. When Cooper had shown up a couple of days later, the situation escalated. They had lost two full days battling one man and one woman.

After the botched attack on the secluded cottage in the Badlands, Cooper and Kemp had disappeared. Liang's men had scoured the countryside searching for any sign of them, but they appeared to have vanished. Liang had sent both Ag Con helicopters out to hunt for them, but they had found nothing. Chen had given Liang until dark to continue the search. After that he was to pull back and use all of his forces to protect the perimeters of both Ag Con facilities.

Chen knew that the time for testing was over. The window for implementing their plans was slamming shut.

It was time for action. He dialed the number of the Kill-deer Mountain lab. "Prepare to disperse the prions," he ordered.

Watford City, North Dakota

GORDON GOULD WANTED nothing more than to kill the goddamned son of a bitch Chen and every one of his goons. No one ordered Gordon Gould around like a house servant. "Go now, please," the little weasel had said.

But when all was said and done, Gould had done as he was told. He also realized that he'd really become a simple houseboy for these people, quite willingly. When Chen had offered Gould $10 million for his services, he would have given the man a happy ending if he had so desired. Ten million dollars would make all of Gould's wildest fantasies reality. It might even be enough to buy a seat in the U.S. Senate. It would be like college, he mused. When Gould was attending the University of North Dakota, he'd bought himself the presidency of the student body simply by purchasing pizza for everyone living in the dorms. That had cost him a little more than a grand.

When Ag Con had opened their facilities in the western part of the state, it seemed like the best thing that had ever happened to Gould. Up until a couple of days ago, Chen and his men had never asked anything of Gould that amounted to more than just greasing a few political wheels. That was the sort of thing Gould did every day in his capacity as president of the North Dakota Cattle Raisers' Association. That included blackmailing Sheriff Buck, but Gould had done the same or worse to several ranchers who opposed the association's programs.

He'd known that Linda was stealing meth from the evidence locker. He knew that because he'd bought it from her, through Jason, of course. He knew everything there was to know about meth in that part of the state because he manufactured most of it. He had a ranch up in Williston where he had a crew of Mexican illegal immigrants cooking it up. He'd manufacture the drug, and his partner, and first cousin, Dan Gould would distribute it. Dan owned several car dealerships in the western part of the state. Once a week Dan and his crew would fly down to Minneapolis to attend the auto auctions. His guys would drive the cars Dan bought back to western North Dakota and Dan would then sell them on his lots. What few people besides Gould knew was that Dan got the money to buy the cars by selling the meth that Gould manufactured. It was a lucrative business, but it was nothing compared to the money Gould was earning from Ag Con.

As Gould drove home from the vet clinic, he wished he'd have been satisfied with the money he earned from his business interests, legitimate and nonlegitimate. It was more than just being berated by the Chinese son of a bitch. Gould had a bad feeling about what was happening. Before Cooper showed up, the Chinese seemed to have everything under control, but the tall stranger had shown him that Ag Con was not omnipotent, despite its army of hired thugs. For the first time, Gould started to worry that he might not have cast his lot with the winning team.

The bad feelings had intensified when he returned to his house. The sheriff's car was still out front, but there were no signs of life inside. He went in but still heard nothing, which was odd, since his speed-freak nephew rarely shut his mouth—and he never slept.

"Is anyone here?" he shouted, but received no answer.

He needed a drink, so he headed to the liquor cabinet in his family room. The first thing he saw when he entered the room was the sheriff's bloated carcass sprawled on his recliner, the back half of his head sprayed across the carpet. He looked over at the other side of the room and saw Jason's body crumpled on the floor in a pool of co-agulated blood.

Then he looked on the floor and saw the empty bottle. "Aw shit," he said, "not the Blue Label." He picked up the bottle—definitely empty. He rummaged around in the liquor cabinet and finally produced a bottle of bour-bon. He put some ice in a tumbler and poured a generous helping of the whiskey into the glass. He needed a drink badly.

He sipped the bourbon and looked at the carnage in the room. For the second time that day he had memo-ries of his time in Vietnam. He'd been a tunnel rat, and he thought he'd seen it all in the time he spent crawl-ing through those tunnels, sometimes over the remains of close friends who'd been blown to bits by bunker-buster bombs, but damned if this wasn't turning out to be worse.

Not that he was heartbroken over Jason dying. He took his nephew under his wing after the boy's father, Gor-don's younger brother, had been killed in a car crash. He felt responsible for his brother's death—he'd gotten him drunk the night he was killed—so he felt obliged to take care of the boy. Since the kid's mother had died of lung cancer a couple years earlier, Gordon and Dan were the only family members Jason had left.

Looking back, Gordon had thought it was a nice touch, getting that video of Linda giving Jason head in the truck. He thought it would soften up the sheriff and make it easier to work with him, but apparently he'd gone too far. He had serious trouble on his hands. All those Build & Berg men that Cooper had been slaughtering were easy enough to deal with. Whatever friends and family they had were half a world away and had no idea their relatives were dying in the barren wastelands of western North Dakota. Ag Con could just dig a ditch and bury them, and no one would ever come looking for them. They probably wouldn't be seen again until years later when some archaeologist came hunting for dinosaur bones.

Jason wasn't much of a problem either. He had run with a rough crowd, and this wouldn't be the first time one of them turned up with a bullet through his head.

The sheriff was a horse of a different color. Even though he'd clearly shot himself, there was bound to be some sort of investigation. That meant that state law-enforcement agents would come around asking questions Gould really didn't want them to ask. They might even bring in the Feds. If only Buck had shot himself in his own damned car instead of in Gould's family room. Inconsiderate bastard, he thought.

Gould finished his bourbon and dialed a number on his cell phone.

"What is it?" Chen asked over the line.

"I got a problem with the sheriff."

"You told me you'd handle the sheriff," Chen said.

"Well, that just turned into a little bit more of a problem then I'd imagined."

"Is he refusing to fill out the report as I requested?" Chen asked.

"He ain't going to be filling out too many reports from here on out. He shot himself in the head."

"He's dead?"

"Most certainly," Gould said, looking at the corpse, which was already starting to swell up.

"How is that a problem?"

"He's dead in the middle of my family room."

"Then let me rephrase my question—how is that my problem?"

"Because there's bound to be an investigation. The powers that be tend to get all bent out of shape when a cop dies, even a fat moron like Jim Buck."

"It seems to me that you would be wise to remove the body from your house then," Chen said.

"I was hoping to get a little help with that."

"All my men are busy at the moment," Chen said. "I suggest you utilize other resources. Your nephew can help you."

"About that," Gould said. "It appears Sheriff Buck shot Jason just before he shot himself."

"I see," Chen said. The connection remained silent for a moment and Gould was afraid he'd lost the call, but just as he was about to hang up and redial Chen said, "I understand the gravity of the situation, but we really cannot spare any men at the moment. Besides, we are paying you handsomely to handle the sheriff. So handle him. Perhaps you should enlist the aid of your partner in the drug business, the car salesman."

5

Kolodziej's request for intel on Matt Cooper had hit a stone wall. There was little of interest to be found. The leader of B&B knew he was on thin ice with his superiors. He didn't know exactly what the price for failure would be, since he'd never failed yet—he didn't want to find out now. Liang had split his forces into four-man squads, and they were beating the sagebrush looking for Cooper and Kemp. Kolodziej's men were doing the same, though he preferred to keep his people in larger squads. He'd seen what Cooper and Kemp could do to twenty men, so he wouldn't risk sending his men out in groups smaller than ten.

Kolodziej had selected his nine best people for his personal team. Usually Kolodziej didn't go into the field, but the circumstances had evolved too far away from the norm to afford him the luxury of staying behind at the Ag Con facility. He had personally recruited all the men in his squad from the ranks of the UOP, and all of them had proved themselves under fire. So far most of those who had died lacked real combat experience. Many of the mercenaries that B&B recruited were killers, but most of the people they had killed had been unarmed villagers in some remote part of the world. Large mining and oil-drilling corporations often hired B&B to remove anything and everything that stood in the way of their operations, and on occasion that included obliterating entire villages.

But this time their prey was fighting back. Kolodziej suspected that many of the people under him had no experience with an adversary who fought back. The men he'd selected for this squad had a very different story to tell. The men in this squad weren't simply bullies who preyed on the helpless—this was a group of trained soldiers.

Not that it mattered, since the odds of any of the squads stumbling across Cooper and Kemp were almost infinitesimally small. It embarrassed Kolodziej to have to resort to this sort of unprofessional and unorganized search-and-destroy mission, but when it came to devising a better plan, both he and Liang were at a loss. They had been given until the end of the day to complete their task, and neither man was willing to accept failure. If they had been able to come up with a better plan, they would have gladly implemented it, but there seemed to be nothing more to do except pick the haystack apart straw by straw in search of the needle.

With such low expectations, it came as something of a shock when he finally did catch a glimpse of the so-called needle. He and his men had been walking down a creek bed that opened into a small canyon in which about thirty head of cattle grazed on the grass along the creek. He'd signaled his men to stop while he crept ahead and scanned the area through his binoculars. On the first pass nothing seemed out of the ordinary, but on the second scan something caught his eye. It was a patch of black. Nothing in nature was black—even a coal seam had a brownish tint to it if you saw it under the sun. Black indicated that a person was looking at some sort of man-made object.

After peering at the black spot for a moment, Kolodziej could make out a couple of perfectly straight horizontal lines. Just as nothing in nature was a true black color, nothing in nature was perfectly straight. He looked at the lines and at the spot of black, and slowly he began to make out the shape of the ATV vehicle in which Cooper and Kemp had escaped. The vehicle had been camouflaged with brush and branches so well that Kolodziej had almost missed it. After studying the surrounding area, he identified a small pile of brush that likely concealed a tent. He'd found his quarry.

Kolodziej studied the terrain and formed a plan of attack. Since there were only two people in the tent, a frontal assault should have sufficed, but his men had tried that tactic twice already, and both times it had ended in devastating failure. They needed a new plan. If they used the creek bed for concealment, his men could get to the cliff wall on the far side of the meadow and make their way toward the encampment along the cliff, where it would be impossible for Cooper and Kemp to see them approach. He'd leave a couple of sharpshooters at this end of the meadow as backup, in case they failed and Cooper and Kemp tried to get away. He quietly ordered the two sharpshooters into position and began to work his way toward the other end of the meadow with the rest of his squad. Kolodziej looked forward to the chance to redeem himself by killing the troublesome pair.

THE SOLDIER AWOKE with a start. He wasn't sure what had awakened him, but his instincts told him something was wrong.

"Wake up," he whispered to Kemp. She started to say

something, but he gently placed his hand over her mouth and whispered, "Something's not right." He donned his holsters and other gear and carefully crept through the tent door, which was facing away from the small meadow. He was careful not to disturb the branches and brush with which they'd covered the tent.

He couldn't identify the sound that had woken him up, but then he realized it was the complete lack of sound that signaled danger. The Badlands might look like a barren wasteland to the untrained eye, but they teemed with life, and where there was life, there were sounds. Whether it was the howling of coyotes or the love song of the —whip-poor-will wooing a potential mate, there were always sounds echoing through the area. The only time the native fauna clammed up was when there was danger present.

Bolan pulled his binoculars from the pouch on his belt and carefully scanned the cliff on the other side of the valley. The sun was getting low in the western sky, to the soldier's back, leaving the wooded draw in which they hid in shadows, but it shone brightly on the far side of the meadow, and he caught a flash of sunlight reflecting off glass. He focused on the spot where he'd seen the flash and saw a man with a scoped rifle pointed their way. But the man wasn't looking directly at Bolan's position; rather, he was focusing on something south of the wooded draw.

The soldier watched the man slowly move his rifle toward Bolan's position. The sharpshooter was watching his comrades as they made their way toward the encampment. From the angle of his gun, Bolan estimated that whoever was coming at them was at least two hundred yards to their south, and not moving terribly quickly.

People could be coming at them from the north, too,

but not likely, since the terrain to the north was virtually impenetrable.

Kemp came out of the tent with her gun and whispered, "What's up?"

"Someone's coming at us from the south, and we've got a sniper watching us from the east. What's above us?"

"More of the same. It's too rugged to pass through. What should we do?"

"I think our best defense might be a good offense, but we can't just pop out and start shooting because the sniper will get us. And he's probably not alone."

"Then what?" she asked.

"Climb as high up the side of the draw as you can get. I'll climb up the other side. Hold your fire until you hear me shoot. Then open up and shoot as fast as you can aim. You take the ones to the east, I'll take the ones to the south. We'll have the advantage of the sun being in their eyes. If we can get them before their eyes adjust to the shadows, we just might survive this."

Kemp scrambled up the south side of the draw, and Bolan climbed up the north. He'd barely gotten into position when the first man crept around the corner and into the draw, then another man appeared, and then another, until six men stood there. They moved toward the tent with remarkable stealth, but they still made noise, and every twig that snapped under their boots echoed through the stone silence of the draw. When the first mercenary reached the point where the sunlight gave way to shadow, Bolan squeezed the trigger on his Browning. A fist-size hole appeared in the center of the man's chest.

Bolan didn't wait to see if the man was dead; he'd already acquired another target and dropped him even before he heard the report from Kemp's Savage. She was fast with the bolt. Bolan squeezed the trigger on his

Browning autoloader as fast as the action could cycle, and he noted that Kemp's second shot came at almost the same moment as his third. Within the space of a second they had dropped five of the six men, but the sixth had dived for cover behind the ATV. Not that the ATV would stop either of their .30-caliber rifles—their bullets would pass through any part of the machine, even the aluminum engine block. But to hit the man they had to see him, and now he had the advantage of being in the dark shadows of the draw.

While Bolan tried to get a bead on the remaining man, he heard the report of a small caliber rifle from the entrance of the draw. Kemp slammed back against the cliff wall she had scaled, and Bolan saw blood appear on her forehead. Before he could determine if she was seriously injured, a hail of bullets chopped up the juniper trunk he'd climbed to get to his position. Bolan pressed himself as flat as he could against the cliff wall, using the tree trunk as cover. From what he could see, there appeared to be two men who had moved just inside the entrance of the draw, both of whom were throwing a lot of lead at Kemp and Bolan. He couldn't make out their exact position because they hid among the rocky outcroppings at the entrance to the ravine.

Bolan heard the report from Kemp's rifle and saw the man who'd taken cover behind the ATV fly from behind the vehicle as if he'd been kicked by a mule. The six-inch exit wound in his back told Bolan that he was out of the fight. It also told him that Kemp was still in it.

But for how long? Their position had been strategically sound for ambushing the main force coming into the draw, but now they were trapped, sitting ducks for the men at the mouth of the draw.

"Cooper," one of the men firing at them shouted, "you cannot escape. Give yourself up."

"Kolodziej?"

"Yes." Kolodziej was startled to hear the soldier shout his name.

Bolan saw that Kemp had crawled to a ledge that ran toward the mouth of the draw. It appeared that she was out of the line of sight of Kolodziej and the other man. Bolan tried to keep him talking to distract him.

"People like you seldom venture into the field. I think you made a mistake," Bolan taunted. "I don't foresee you living much longer."

"It doesn't seem to me that you're in any position to end my life," Kolodziej stated.

"I'm not," Bolan said. He looked and saw that Kemp was just about in position to take a shot. "But perhaps I don't have to be."

Kemp aimed down at Kolodziej and squeezed off a shot. As his partner swung upward to fire back at her, Bolan leaned out and drilled the man with his BAR.

"We got them!" Kemp shouted.

"Are you all right?" Bolan asked.

"I got a gash across my forehead and I'm bleeding like a stuck pig, but if I can get this cleaned up it won't leave much of a scar."

"We can't start cleaning up just yet," Bolan said. "We need to deal with that sniper. Maybe with a couple of snipers."

"I've got an idea," Kemp said.

CHEN'S SAT PHONE rang and he saw that Liang was calling. "What have you to report?" he asked.

"Kolodziej just contacted me. He said he'd found Cooper and Kemp."

"Where are they?" Chen asked. Liang relayed the GPS coordinates that the Polish man had given him. "What was Kolodziej going to do?"

"He said he was taking eight men to attack them at their campsite. He'd left two men guarding the entrance to the site in case things go wrong."

"Kolodziej is good," Chen said, "but I'm afraid Mr. Cooper is better. What do you plan to do to resolve the situation?"

"I've ordered both helicopters to the location right away. Each has eight men aboard. They should be at the campsite within half an hour."

Chen thought about that for a moment, and then said, "Call the helicopters back."

"Are you certain?" Liang asked. "We are on the verge of capturing Cooper."

"I'm afraid you may be on the verge of simply losing more men," Chen replied. "So far all of your efforts to capture Cooper have been worse than ineffectual. We have lost an astounding number of men in an effort to capture two individuals. It is time to cut our losses. I want you to call off the search, fall back and focus your efforts on protecting the facilities."

"I respectfully disagree," Liang said. "This man is cagey. We should not underestimate him. As long as he remains out of our grasp, he poses a threat to our enterprise."

"I agree that he is a wily opponent," Chen said, "but we need the helicopters to transport the product from the laboratory to the feed-grinding facility in Iowa."

"What?" Liang asked. "We weren't going to deploy the product for at least another two weeks. We haven't completed testing."

"We no longer have the luxury of completing the tests,"

Chen said. "These attacks we've been experiencing mean that someone somewhere knows too much about our activities. Even if we defeat Cooper, there will be more where he came from. But if we can deploy the product and get it into the food supply, there will be nothing an army of Coopers can do to stop us."

"I understand, sir, but please allow us this one last chance to capture Cooper. We are sending the very best men we have after him this time."

"From what I've seen your best might not be good enough," Chen said.

"Please, sir. Between Kolodziej's men on the ground and my troops approaching in the helicopters, Cooper faces impossible odds this time."

"I am willing to compromise," Chen said. "Recall the helicopters and allow Kolodziej and his men to proceed against Cooper."

"Sir, I respectfully believe that would be a mistake. I believe we will need my men to attack from the air to deliver the coup de grâce."

Chen remained silent, pondering Liang's proposal. "I will allow you to use one helicopter. I need to begin loading the product onto the other helicopter immediately. If I have your assurance that you will send one helicopter to the Killdeer Mountain facility, I will allow you to use the other in your campaign against Cooper."

After Liang had assured Chen that he would recall one helicopter, Chen returned to his conversation with Zoeng Wei, the geneticist heading the research team at the laboratory. The man seemed unwilling to alter his program in the face of the new reality.

"We have not finished testing," Zoeng said. "We will not be ready for several weeks."

"Will the prions work as needed in their current state?"

"Yes, but the timing is still too unpredictable. Encephalopathy might take anywhere from two weeks to a month to develop. With a little more time, we can make the timing more precise."

"We do not have the luxury of more time," Chen said. "A two-week window is more than adequate. Is enough of the product ready?"

"We've infected several hundred kilos of finely ground animal protein with vast amounts of prions," Zoeng said. "At a rate of ten grams of infected protein to one metric ton of feed, we should have enough to infect approximately thirty thousand metric tons of feed."

"That's not as much as we had hoped for," Chen said.

"If we had several more weeks to work on the program, we could have one hundred times that amount available."

"As I said, we do not have several more weeks. Besides, thirty thousand metric tons is more than enough to poison a large portion of the nation's beef supply. If we distribute it properly, we should still be able to infect well over a million animals, which should translate into millions of fatalities. It may not kill as many people as we had originally hoped, but it will have the desired effect of bringing the U.S. economy to a halt and throwing its entire system into chaos. How soon can you have the product ready for transport?"

"With adequate manpower, two days," Zoeng said.

"What is involved?"

"We need to transport the product in sealed casks. It is far too dangerous to transport by any other method. Breathe in one prion particle, and you will soon die a horrible death. We have already lost several people to Creutzfeldt-Jakob disease. It will take at least two days to safely load the existing product into the casks."

"You have twelve hours," Chen replied. "Please, do not disappoint me."

WHILE KEMP'S IDEA was a bit unorthodox, Bolan had to admit that it just might work. The sniper, or snipers, had them pinned down. The rifles that Kolodziej and his men carried were equipped with ATN night-vision scopes, meaning that the snipers in the trees very likely carried the same equipment. He'd had to leave the DPMS with the FLIR back at the vet clinic when he and Kemp had fled in the ATV. That equipment would have more than evened the odds, but Bolan had to make do with the night-scope-equipped QBZ rifles he'd confiscated from the merce-naries for him and Kemp. He'd managed to scavenge ten 30-round magazines for each of them. Kemp traded her Savage bolt gun for the QBZ, but Bolan hung on to the Browning in case he needed more firepower than the compact Chinese rifle could provide.

Even though Bolan and Kemp had upgraded their optics, the snipers still had the advantage of knowing where they were, while Bolan had only a general loca-tion for one sniper and no idea if there were more, and if so, how many. Kemp's plan was low-tech, but it still might work. When the shooting had started, the cattle milling around in the meadow near the entrance of the wooded draw had dispersed, but once it died down, they'd returned to eat the thicker grass that grew along the creek bed. Kemp's idea was to use the cattle as cover to escape the snipers.

Bolan was studying the situation, plotting a route to the cattle that would give him the most cover from the snipers, when he heard the helicopter approaching. Kemp heard it, too. "What do we do now?" she asked.

"We can't go out, so we don't have much choice but to go up."

They scrambled back up the side of the draw, using branches and exposed juniper roots for footholds and handholds, until they reached an outcropping that jutted away from the cliff, creating a small space in which they could hide from anyone above them using night-vision optics. Bolan didn't have to tell Kemp to press herself as tightly against the cliff wall as possible—she was already doing it. He hoped the ledge above them jutted far enough to block their heat signatures from the eyes in the sky.

It stuck out far enough to block the helicopter from Bolan's view, even when he could hear it almost directly above them. The soldier hoped the reverse was also true. They would soon find out, because someone opened up with a heavy-caliber machine gun and tracer rounds lit up the night. Bolan guessed that they had to be using a pintle-mounted gun from inside the door, as he hadn't seen any fixed weapons on the outside of the helicopters that had taken away Bowman and Grevoy. The shots were too steady to be coming from a handheld weapon.

The machine-gun fire pulverized the ATV and shredded the tent to bits. Bolan still couldn't see the helicopter, but he knew he was correct that it was nearly on top of them when he saw the ropes fall down mere yards from their position. As soon as the first person began descending the rope, Bolan raised his QBZ rifle and shot the man. The man lost his grip on his ascender and fell to the ground. By this time several more men had begun to descend the ropes. Bolan managed to tag two more, and Kemp nailed one, but four made it down to the bottom of the draw. The soldier plugged one through the top of his head and Kemp dropped a second, but the remaining two managed to scramble away. Bolan lost sight of them in the dark.

Meanwhile the helicopter was trying to maneuver down into the draw to enable the door gunner to get a fix on Bolan and Kemp's position, but there wasn't quite enough room to get the big, refurbished Huey low enough for an accurate shot. The pilot did manage to get low enough for Bolan to put a bead on the windshield right about where the pilot should be sitting in the cockpit. The Executioner had switched to the Browning, and emptied the 4-round magazine into the cockpit. He was glad he'd slung both rifles because the powerful .30-caliber bullet the Browning spit out would do a lot more damage through Plexiglas than the 5.56 mm bullet the QBZ fired. The nose of the helicopter rose up, then tilted back down and the helicopter slammed into the bottom of the draw, its rotors chopping everything within their seventeen-meter diameter to pulp. Bolan hoped that included the two men who had gotten away.

The soldier scanned the area below through the night scope on the QBZ and saw a hot smear beneath one of the broken helicopter rotors and heat signatures from what looked like scattered body parts. That accounted for one of the men on the ground. He scanned the helicopter wreckage and saw heat signatures from two slumped forms in the cockpit. They weren't moving, and Bolan could tell from their fading heat signatures that their body temperatures were dropping. Both were dead.

Bolan caught movement in the rear area of the cockpit. It was the door gunner. He was trying to get to the gun, which had come to rest on its side, pointing upward out of the helicopter—aimed. The gun was pointed almost directly at him and Kemp. Bolan sighted the ATN scope on the figure and squeezed off a short full-auto burst. He scored a direct hit and the figure stopped moving.

Shots rang out from below, and several bullets ricocheted off the ledge just above them. Before Bolan could get a location on the shooter, Kemp had drawn a bead on him and fired her QBZ. The soldier looked through his scope toward where she'd fired and saw a figure slumped on the ground. She'd nailed him.

When they were certain no one was left alive amid the wreckage, Bolan and Kemp made their way back down to what remained of their campsite. They salvaged a few items, restocked their ammo and prepared to implement Kemp's escape plan.

LIANG HELD the sat phone in his hand without answering until it stopped vibrating. When he was unable to contact Kolodziej, he began to worry. The B&B mercenaries varied as widely in their abilities as they did in their countries of origin, but the contingent that Kolodziej selected for his squadron were the best of the lot, roughly comparable to the men he'd hand-selected from the most highly trained members of the People's Liberation Army special forces for this mission. It seemed inconceivable that Cooper would be able to defeat Kolodziej and his crew.

As impossible as it was to believe that a lone man could defeat a squadron of highly trained and experienced soldiers, Liang found the fact that he'd lost contact with the helicopter filled with his own men even more difficult to grasp. The colonel could only assume the worst. He knew that fast thinking and tactical brilliance could hold off overwhelming force to a point, but he had never before encountered an opponent like Cooper.

Chen had been tolerant of the situation up until now, mostly because he was preoccupied with implementing the program on which they had been working these long months, but Liang knew that Chen's patience was wearing thin. The man was going to be furious about the loss of the helicopter, and there wasn't time to procure another.

Chen had acquiesced and allowed him a final attempt to capture or kill Cooper. He would not allow him another.

The colonel felt the sat phone in his hand vibrate again, he slid it into the drop pouch attached to his right leg. Chen wanted an update on the operations against Cooper. Once Liang reported what he knew, which admittedly was just that things seemed to have gone horribly wrong again, Chen would order him back to the Ag Con facilities. But Liang wasn't about to accept failure. At this point he knew that bringing back the lifeless bodies of Cooper and Kemp would be the only thing that would redeem him in Chen's eyes.

Liang and the three men who'd been in his patrol careened down the oil-field road that passed closest to the location in which Kolodziej had located Cooper and Kemp. Liang drove the cumbersome SUV as fast as the oversize truck could go without sliding off the rough, dusty road. Another SUV filled with more men followed him, but the driver could not maintain the pace that Liang set and it gradually receded in Liang's rearview mirror.

He approached the trail that led to the pasture and drove right through the barbed-wire gate, which snapped in an explosion of stretched barbed wire. Liang followed the trail as far as was possible in a full-size vehicle, stopping a little more than a kilometer south of the GPS coordinates that Kolodziej had sent him after the man had identified Cooper's campsite. Liang's men were out of the vehicle and had donned their gear by the time the second SUV pulled up.

"Quickly," Liang ordered the men in the second vehicle, "prepare to move out."

The colonel studied the topographic map of the area on his GPS unit and plotted his course of action. A creek had carved out a small canyon, the bottom of which opened up a bit just north of their location to form a small meadow. That was where Cooper had encountered Kolodziej's and Liang's men in the helicopter. The western side of the canyon ended in a steep cliff that rose to give way to approximately six miles of some of the most rugged Badlands in the entire region. The eastern edge of the meadow ended in steep hills covered with sage and juniper, Liang knew. That was where Kolodziej had left the sharpshooters, who would probably still be in position, if Cooper hadn't managed to kill them, too. He had no way of contacting them, since all their communications were filtered through Kolodziej. The best possible outcome right now would be for the sharpshooters to kill Cooper and Kemp and bring this travesty of an operation to an end.

The snipers should be able to kill their quarry, or at the very least keep the cursed pair boxed in the canyon while they awaited reinforcements, but the events of the past several days had taught Liang the danger of assuming anything when it came to Cooper. After studying the topography, he decided the best course of action would be to leave half his forces to guard the bottleneck at the south end of the canyon where the only way to get out was a seventy-yard stretch of grassland through which the creek ran. Liang and the other three men would make their way along the eastern edge of the canyon and try to make contact with the sharpshooters. What the colonel did after that would be determined by what he learned from the snipers—if they were still alive.

6

Bolan knew Kemp's plan was a long shot at best, but he couldn't think of a better one. They'd crept along the edge of the wooded draw and hid behind an outcropping where the ravine gave way to the meadow. The large rocks provided cover from the sniper, or snipers, in the trees on the other side of the meadow, but their position could quickly become as much of a trap as a refuge. Bolan chanced a peek through the ATN scope and made out the edges of a heat signature among what had to have been juniper trees.

As he looked at the figure on the other side of the creek bed, trying to estimate the distance, Bolan saw a bright flare from the heat signature across the meadow. Before he heard the report, he saw sod fly up where the bullet hit the ground several feet in front of their position. The sniper had seen his heat signature through his identical scope and had taken a shot at Bolan, forcing the soldier to take cover behind the rocks. Judging from the amount of bullet drop, Bolan estimated that the sniper was at least four hundred yards away from their position, though probably closer to five hundred yards. It would be difficult for the sniper to get a fix on Bolan and Kemp's position, but not impossible, and given that the sniper had a better estimate of the distance between them, he would be able to get an accurate shot at them before Bolan could get an accurate shot at him.

The cattle had been closing in on the meadow in front of the wooded draw. When the sniper fired, he'd startled the animals, but the report of the round hadn't been loud enough to scatter the herd, as had happened when Bolan had fought with Kolodziej's forces. "You think you can get these animals to cooperate with us?" Bolan asked Kemp.

"I can get Earl to cooperate with me when I harvest his semen," Kemp said.

"Well, I guess if you can get Earl to go along with that, you can probably get these heifers to work with us," he said. "But we have to wait until they get right up to the edge of the draw. If we try to move from here without cover, we're dead."

"What do we do until then?" Kemp asked.

"Make ourselves as comfortable as possible behind these rocks. When the time comes, we're going to have to move, and move fast. You'll want as much blood circulating in your limbs as possible." There wasn't much space to stretch out behind the cover of the rocks. Kemp and Bolan shifted around until they were in a position that could best be described as "spooning."

"If I liked men, this might seem romantic," Kemp said, commenting on the intimate nature of their position.

"Hiding from someone who's trying to kill you would sort of dampen a person's ardor," Bolan said.

"Good point."

"THESE HEIFERS MIGHT be a problem," Kemp said after twenty minutes had passed. The herd grazing in the meadow consisted of heifers and their calves, which appeared to be just about ready for weaning. "For most of them, it looks like these are their first calves. Heifers can get a little crazy and overprotective with their first calves."

Bolan looked at the heifers. They probably weighed at least six hundred pounds each, if not more. He could see where an animal that size getting "a little crazy" might cause a problem. "So how do we do this?" he asked.

"When they get close enough to block our heat signatures from our friend over there—" Kemp nodded toward the sniper's position "—we crawl out and mingle in with the herd."

"Then what?" Bolan asked.

"That's a good question. I suppose we can try one of two things. We can attempt to coax the entire herd to move toward the south, where we can make it to the trail we came in on."

"What's the other option?" Bolan asked.

"You can shoot that son of a bitch, but that presents its own set of problems. First off, it will make the heifers scatter, so we'll lose our cover and be sitting ducks. Second, if there're more of them out there, it will let them know exactly where we are."

"Maybe we can try a combination of the two plans," Bolan said. "We mix in with the herd, keeping close to the animals so that the sniper can't distinguish our heat signals from theirs, but instead of trying to coax them all the way out of the meadow, we try to get them to move to the east, where I can maybe see if there are other shooters out there and get a better shot at them."

"If I had a better idea," Kemp said, "I'd say you were insane, but I don't see a lot of options."

ANDREJ ZAJAC HAD watched the firefight in the wooded draw, never doubting that Kolodziej and the rest of the squad would defeat the man and woman hiding in the brush. But Zajac could see that the battle hadn't gone as planned for his comrades—some of them had already been killed. But he could still see Kolodziej and another man standing just outside the entrance to the ravine. When the gunfire started to die down, he watched as Kolodziej and the other man moved forward, but then Zajac lost sight of them among the boulders strewed around at the mouth of the ravine.

Seconds later Zajac heard the report from two rounds fired by the large-caliber hunting rifles carried by their prey—the sound of their guns was easy to distinguish from the 5.56 mm NATO rounds his comrades fired. After that Zajac heard and saw nothing, but from the silence of his handheld radio, he guessed that the last two shots had taken out Kolodziej and the other man.

This was just the contingency for which Kolodziej had placed Zajac and his partner in their sniping positions. He regretted that Kolodziej had apparently been killed because the man had been a strong leader, but he felt little on a personal level. Theirs was a business in which it was best not to develop close friendships and personal relationships. Kolodziej had given Zajac a task to do in case Kolodziej and his men failed to kill the Americans, and now that they had indeed failed, Zajac would perform his task as directed.

But when Zajac heard the helicopter coming, he thought he would no longer have to perform the task of eliminating the Americans. Liang's men would certainly overwhelm the Americans, though Zajac was surprised to see just one helicopter arrive on the scene. He would have expected Liang to come after the Americans with all the forces he could marshal.

The sun was setting when the helicopter flew in. Twilight was the time when the optics on his rifle were the least useful. During the bright hours of the day he kept a pinhole shade over the lens to keep the night-vision circuitry from being overwhelmed by too much light, and at night he removed the shade for full night-vision capabilities. The dim light available when the sun set or rose was too bright to allow Zajac to remove the pinhole shade, but it did not provide enough light to adequately illuminate the images through the pinhole.

Since his scope was virtually useless when the helicopter arrived, Zajac watched the events unfold with his naked eyes. But he could barely believe what he saw when he watched the helicopter crash into the ravine.

Regardless of how shocking the turn of events was, it didn't change Zajac's assignment. He looked over at Kazmierz Grabowski, his partner to the south. Grabowski's job was to kill the Americans if they made it past Zajac and attempted to leave the canyon via the trail that ran along the creek bed. Grabowski appeared to be trying to see what had happened, but from his position he couldn't have seen anything after the helicopter dipped into the ravine.

After the helicopter crashed, Zajac waited and watched for anyone trying to escape from the ravine. The fact that he hadn't heard anything over his radio meant that if anyone was alive in the ravine, it could only be the Americans, which in turn meant that it was his job to shoot anyone trying to escape. Zajac had been trained as a sniper for Grupa Reagowania Operacyjno-Manewrowego— GROM—Poland's version of the U.S. SOCOM forces. He had waited for days for a target to appear in his sights. He knew that the Americans hiding in the cliffs across from his position did not have days to wait. He knew that Liang and his Chinese troops would eventually arrive to finish what Kolodziej and his men had started.

Zajac's waiting eventually paid off. After watching the entrance to the ravine for approximately half an hour after the helicopter crashed, he saw a faint heat signature appear from behind a boulder at the edge of the ravine. Before the sun had set he'd estimated the distance to the center of the ravine, where the campsite was located, and he'd also gauged the distance to the entrance of the ravine. But it was difficult to measure the exact distance to the boulders just inside the mouth of the ravine. He made his best guess, adjusted his aim to compensate and fired at the heat signature. His bullet hit about a meter in front of the target, which meant he would have to aim a bit higher the next time the target appeared.

With the proper gear, Zajac would have made short work of the Americans, but the optics on his rifle were far from ideal for this sort of sniping work, as was the rifle itself. The bullpup design made it a compact and maneuverable combat rifle, but the long link between the trigger and the sear made the trigger break with a spongy feel that impeded accuracy. When equipped with a night scope like the ATN, the QBZ was ideal for close-quarters combat, but far from ideal for sniping.

Still, Zajac had been trained to work with the equipment he had available, and the next time his targets presented themselves, he felt he stood a much better chance of scoring a hit. He was preparing for such a shot when the cattle began to move into his field of fire. He watched closely to see if any two-legged creatures moved among the animals, but it was difficult to distinguish between their heat signatures and any human signatures moving among them.

When the cattle became too much of an impediment to watching his prey, Zajac decided to take drastic action; he picked out an animal in the midst of the herd and shot it, hoping to scatter the animals.

BOLAN AND KEMP had just crept in among the heifers when the sniper fired a shot. Bolan looked to see if Kemp, who was about fifteen feet to the soldier's right, had been hit, but she appeared unharmed. A heifer about thirty yards to the soldier's left wasn't so lucky. Bolan watched the animal stagger, then drop to its front knees and roll onto its side. The cattle immediately surrounding it appeared startled, but the herd didn't panic.

Kemp stood up and crouched beside a heifer, startling it a bit, but her manner and familiarity with cattle calmed the animal. She motioned for Bolan to do the same. Instead of standing, the soldier remained on his belly, looking between the legs of the heifer in front of him to see what the sniper was doing. It appeared that the sniper was scanning the area, looking for targets. The shot had to have been designed to get the animals to clear out from the area so that the man could get a better view of the wooded draw.

Then Bolan took Kemp's cue and stood up. Kemp was using her body language to manipulate the heifer. She clearly had a lot of experience working with these animals, moving slowly and smoothly, not fast enough or aggressively enough to startle the heifer she was using for cover, but with sufficient presence to command the animal to walk slowly away from her. Bolan recognized her movements as a variation of the tactic border collies used to herd cattle. Kemp moved at the same pace as the heifer, using it as a shield to block her heat signature from the sniper. Bolan copied her movements and the heifer in front of him began to slowly move away from him, but he quickly figured out how to control the direction of the heifer through the positioning of his own body.

The system worked fairly well for a while, and he and Kemp were able to make the animals they were using for cover move nearly one hundred yards closer to the sniper's position before the man once again fired into the herd. The report was considerably louder this much closer to its source, and the noise startled the cattle in the vicinity, including the two heifers Bolan and Kemp used for cover. Kemp dived to the ground, and Bolan dropped to a shooting position and found the sniper in the crosshairs of his scope. The sniper's attention was still focused on the region in front of the draw, and Bolan was able to get off a shot before the shooter realized that his prey was much closer than he'd anticipated.

Bolan could see that he'd scored a hit, but it wasn't a killing shot. The sniper returned fire, though his injuries seemed to affect his aim. Bolan and Kemp were within yards of the creek bed, which was mostly dry, except for a trickle of water running along the bottom.

"Run for the creek!" Bolan shouted to Kemp. The woman was closer to the creek and reached it first. The sniper squeezed off a few more shots at the pair as they ran, but again his aim was off and he was unable to connect with the moving targets.

The soldier jumped into the creek bed and found Kemp already there. "Are you all right?" he asked.

"Yeah," she said.

Bolan crept to the bank and chanced a peek over the top—he was rewarded with a shot from the sniper. This one missed the soldier's head by inches, indicating that the sniper had regained his composure, at least to some degree.

There wasn't much for cover in the meadow, but about one hundred yards to the south stood a large outcropping that rose at least six feet above the meadow grass. Beyond that the terrain became increasingly rugged, until it gave way to the hills in the east where the sniper was located.

"Follow me," Bolan said. He ran in a crouch along the creek bed until the outcropping was directly between them and the sniper. The man had to have seen that they were moving, maybe catching a glimpse of their heat signatures, because he fired a few shots. They went wild.

Bolan again inched up to the edge of the creek bed. He couldn't see the shooter, and hoped that meant that the man couldn't see them, either. He scanned the area, and for the first time caught sight of a second sniper. The man appeared to be looking at his partner through his night-vision scope, probably trying to see how severely the first man had been wounded. Bolan took the opportunity to take a shot at the second sharpshooter. This time Bolan's shot appeared to be more effective—the man lay on the ground, not moving. The Executioner scanned the area looking for another shooter, but found nothing.

"Stay here," he told Kemp and crept to the rocks rising up from the grass. He crawled around the edge of the stones, until he got a glimpse of the sniper through his night-vision scope. The man was still scanning the creek bed and appeared to be having difficulty moving. Bolan was much closer this time, and when he fired, his bullet hit the target directly in his center of mass. The sniper slumped against the tree he'd been using as a hide and didn't move.

Bolan scanned the area to the south, looking for more snipers. Just when he thought they were going to make it out of the canyon alive, he saw the heat signatures of four men coming through the narrow opening of the canyon.

"Are we safe?" Kemp asked when the soldier came back to her position in the creek bed.

"No. We're getting company from the south. I think you should round up some manure?"

LIANG AND HIS MEN were just about ready to leave the vehicles when they heard the first shot. "Hurry!" he ordered them. When he was positioning the squad at the entrance of the canyon, he heard a second shot.

"Follow me!" he shouted and ran in a crouch along the cliff that opened up into the meadow.

Once inside the canyon he looked through the night-vision scope on his rifle in an attempt to locate the position of the sharpshooters that Kolodziej had placed along the eastern edge of the canyon. He spotted one a bit more than a half a mile north of their position. The man lay prone, not moving, and was most likely dead. Perhaps three hundred yards north of the dead man he saw the second sniper. The man was upright, but didn't appear to be moving. From this distance he couldn't tell if the man was alive or not. He scanned the rest of the area, but was unable to detect the heat signatures of anything but the cattle grazing in the meadow.

Liang and his troops ran as fast as they could with their gear and reached the first sharpshooter. As Liang had suspected, the man had been killed, but judging from the amount of fresh blood still pouring from the bullet wound, the man had only been dead ten or twenty minutes, at most, perhaps less. Again Liang scanned the meadow, and again the only heat signatures he picked up came off the cattle. From this position he could see that the second sharpshooter also appeared to be either dead or severely injured. If he was wounded, his injuries would be mortal if for no other reason than the fact that Liang wasn't going to expend the resources to tend to them.

After scanning the field once again, he saw what he thought could be the only possible hiding place for Cooper and Kemp—the ravine where Kolodziej had first spotted them. Liang and his men ran to the entrance of the ravine, stopping several times along the way to scan for their quarry, in case they were somewhere that he hadn't been able to see from his previous position.

On one of those stops he thought he might have picked up a heat signature that didn't belong to a cow, but upon closer study it appeared as though the heat was generated from a rather large pile of fresh manure and Liang and his men continued moving toward the entrance of the ravine.

When they approached the ravine, Liang scanned its interior with his night-vision scope. He was able to make out the faint and rapidly fading heat signatures of many, many bodies, but saw no sign of anyone still alive. The men cautiously approached the entrance, watching for any sign of ambush, but all they encountered was carnage. Kolodziej had died within yards of the entrance to the ravine. The bodies of Kolodziej's mercenaries were intermingled with the bodies of Liang's own commandos, and in the center of the chaotic scene lay the wreckage of the helicopter.

Liang's men spread out and searched the scene, looking for signs of Cooper or Kemp, but found only the remains of their own men. Not one remained alive. The scene looked very much like hell might. It seemed impossible that one man and one woman could have been responsible for this much destruction. It looked more like his men had awakened some sort of demonic presence.

Once he was satisfied that Cooper and Kemp weren't in

the ravine, Liang ordered his men back into the meadow and began looking for other possible hiding locations. He contemplated the possibility of their heading north into the heart of the Badlands, but if that was the case, the pair wouldn't emerge until after Chen had carried out his plans—if they emerged at all. It would take several days for even a supersoldier like Cooper to make it through that terrain.

Liang was scanning the meadow one last time when he heard the shots from the south.

KEMP HADN'T BEEN enthusiastic about Bolan's plan for the two of them to cover themselves in mud and manure to obscure their heat signatures, but instead of arguing with her, he began covering himself with a foul mixture of the two substances, caking it on as thickly as possible. When Kemp saw Bolan was serious, she too began covering herself with mud and manure. There was no shortage of either substance in the creek bed.

The plan seemed to have worked. As the Ag Con goons made their way north toward the snipers' locations, Cooper and Kemp crawled south along the creek bed. Cooper knew that this cheap trick wouldn't fool potent night-vision optics like the FLIR that he'd left back at Kemp's veterinarian clinic, but the ATN was a combat optic, designed to provide a certain amount of night-vision capabilities while at the same time providing a wide field of vision with a clear view of the surrounding area and the ability to acquire targets quickly. It was an excellent combat scope, but its ability to spot heat signatures was minimal, making it possible to disguise a heat signature with some sort of protective covering. Such as manure and mud.

At one point Bolan feared that they hadn't disguised

themselves well enough to fool the ATN optics. He chanced a look back through his own ATN scope and saw that the men had stopped and one appeared to be looking directly at them through his rifle optics. Bolan signaled Kemp to remain still until the man finally stopped looking their way and continued on toward the wooded draw.

By the time the men entered the valley, Bolan and Kemp were within three hundred yards of the narrow opening into the canyon. The soldier scanned the area beyond the entrance and saw two men posted on the west side of the trail. He was willing to bet money that at least two more men were located on the east side, too. He motioned for Kemp to come up beside him.

"I want you to crawl to the rocks near the east side of the canyon entrance," he told her. "There are two men on the west side of the trail. I want you to remain prone, but target one of the men. I'm going to the west side of the opening. My guess is that there are at least two more men out there. Wait until you hear my shot, then shoot the man in your sights and try to take out the second as fast as possible."

Kemp didn't say a word and just crawled into position. By the time she got there, Bolan had already assumed his spot. She'd barely gotten her crosshairs centered on the first of her targets when she heard Bolan shoot. He'd switched his weapon to full-auto and was spraying his side of the road, but Kemp kept her rifle on the single-round setting. It had been a long time since she'd fired a rifle set on full-auto, and she wasn't sure she could handle it. She squeezed the trigger of her gun and her target went down. She heard Bolan continue to spray autofire at his targets while she pumped a single round into her second target. He too dropped, but she saw that the first man had sat back up and was returning fire on her position. She put the crosshairs on his chest, but her third shot went a little high. Even so, it was effective. She saw the top of the man's head fly backward, but he remained seated, and even managed to squeeze off another shot, though it was unaimed and went wild. She'd already fired a third round into the man before she realized he was either dead or close to it.

A few days earlier she would never have thought that she'd ever be able take a human life. Now she was doing it as if it was a hobby, like knitting a sweater or playing golf. It was too much to process.

Bolan's shouts broke her from her thoughts. "Move!" he shouted. "Now!"

Kemp ran as fast as her legs could carry her, which was amazingly fast. She may have been tiny but she was strong, fit, and she kept up with Bolan's explosive pace fairly well.

Kemp ran hard until the trail widened and she saw two parked SUVs. They were black Chevrolet Tahoes, the kind that Ag Con employees drove. Bolan was already hot-wiring the closer of the two by the time Kemp arrived, and had it revving before the woman finished scrambling into the cab. Just as he slammed the vehicle into Reverse and stomped on the accelerator, a stream of bullets crashed through the windshield. Bolan threw himself down onto the seat, pulling Kemp down with him, all the while holding the accelerator to the floor. He cranked the wheel, and the truck whipped around so that the front end was facing away from the approaching shooters. He slammed the gearshift lever into Drive, and once again floored the accelerator as bullets burst through the rear window of the vehicle.

"Buckle your seat belt," Bolan told Kemp. "This is going to be one hell of a ride."

CHEN LOOKED at the sat phone and shook his head. Liang had been a good captain, perhaps the best with which he had ever worked, but when he failed to answer his phone, Chen could only assume one of two things.

The first, of course, was that Liang was dead. Given the body count that Cooper had racked up in the past several days, Chen realized that it was a distinct possibility. But there was also another possibility: that Liang's pride in his work had turned to hubris and the man had chosen to willfully disobey Chen rather than concede defeat.

Either reality meant that the Cooper situation had yet to be settled. It also most likely meant that Liang's men had lost the helicopter. Chen couldn't imagine how a single man—and of course his veterinarian sidekick—could hold out against at least twenty highly trained soldiers who had the advantage of air support, but that appeared to be what had happened.

Chen tried once again to reach Liang, and once again Liang failed to answer his sat phone. He was going to have to arrange some other form of transit to the Iowa facility. There was no room aboard the helicopter hauling the product, which would already be overloaded with just the containers of product and the pilot. Plus it would be dangerous—Chen did not want to be breathing air in which the prions were stored, even if they were kept in sealed casks. In the course of their research they had lost six technicians because of exposure to the product, and that was after taking every conceivable precaution.

Now he regretted not renewing the lease on Ag Con's corporate jet. He had made the decision to let the jet go after the U.S. auto industry meltdown had turned private jets into symbols of corporate greed. For Ag Con to fulfill its mission, Chen and his partners had needed to keep as low a profile as possible. Anything that might draw unwanted attention to the corporation would have been counterproductive.

Commercial travel was also out of the question. Chen didn't know who Cooper worked for, but the man had to have connections with a security organization of some sort. Chen had no idea how encompassing was the reach of this organization, but he could not take the chance that he had been put on some sort of terrorist watch list. Commercial air travel was not an option—he would definitely have to make other arrangements.

Chen knew one person who had a private plane that was easily capable of transporting him quickly and safely to the Ag Con facilities in Iowa. He once again reached for his sat phone and dialed a number. When he heard the voice on the other end, he said, "Mr. Gould, are you making progress dealing with the remains of the sheriff?" From the hysterical, incoherent response, Chen gathered that Gould still had not solved his problem. "Is your cousin the drug peddler helping you?" He was. "I think I can free up the resources to solve your dilemma, but in return I will need your cousin to perform a service for me."

7

When Liang heard the shots coming from the entrance to the canyon, he knew that Cooper and Kemp had somehow slipped past his men as they'd made their way to the ravine. The group ran back toward the squad Liang had left at the south end of the canyon. When they reached the squad, all four men appeared to be dead, but Liang didn't stop to check; he kept running after Cooper and Kemp. When he and his men approached the area where they'd been forced to abandon their vehicles, Liang saw one of the SUVs starting to drive away.

Liang raised his rifle and fired a full-auto blast at the fleeing vehicle. He saw the windshield shatter beneath the spray of bullets, but the vehicle kept going backward at a high rate of speed. The driver cranked the wheel and the vehicle changed directions in a swirl of dust. Liang fired into the dust cloud, and when the vehicle emerged from the other side, he saw that he had taken out the rear window as well as the front.

He and his men ran for the remaining SUV, but when they got there, they realized that the key for the vehicle resided with one of the dead men at the mouth of the canyon. Liang sent one of his gunners to retrieve it. The man returned in a very short time, but to Liang the wait seemed eternal. Killing Cooper and Kemp had become his obsession, and it had caused him to lose all sense of proportion.

When the man returned with the key, Liang started the vehicle and drove down the rough trail at such a high speed that he risked breaking the suspension components of the vehicle. Even though they all wore seat belts, the men inside the cab were tossed about so hard that the three without the good fortune of having a steering wheel for a handhold hit their heads against the windows with almost concussive force.

The trail wound down through a valley and back up some hills on the other side. The trail of dust that Cooper's vehicle kicked up hung over the valley like a fog. Cooper had turned off the headlights of his vehicle, but even though it was a moonless night, the stars shone so brightly that there was enough light for navigation. Cooper had no way of turning off his brake lights, and Liang saw them light up as the vehicle crested the hills ahead of them.

Liang estimated that it was approximately one mile to the point where he'd seen the brake lights come on. The trail connected with the oil-field road just over the crest of the hill ahead. The brake lights indicated that Cooper had just turned onto the oil-field road at the spot where Liang had crashed through the gate earlier.

Liang was traveling at seventy miles per hour. That meant that he was only a minute or two behind Cooper. He pushed the accelerator closer to the floorboards and increased his speed to eighty miles per hour, hoping the vehicle would withstand such punishment.

When Liang reached the crest of the hill, the turn onto

the oil-field road took him by surprise. He had underestimated his speed, and when he cranked the wheel the truck slid broadside across the road and down in the shallow ditch that ran alongside the road. The SUV continued through a fence that bordered the ditch. Liang cranked the wheel of the vehicle back toward the road and stabbed the accelerator to the floor. He aimed for a spot between two fence poles and punched his way through the fence and up the bank.

Once on the road he increased the speed to 105 mph, which seemed to be the lumbering truck's top speed. At that rate he could barely keep the vehicle on the narrow road. His task was made more difficult by the trail of dust hanging over the road, reducing visibility to nearly zero.

At least the dust cloud told him he was on the right track. When Liang burst through the cloud into clean air, he knew he'd lost his quarry. He slammed on the brakes, nearly sliding back off the road as he came to a stop. His wheels dug so deeply into the loose scoria that had been used for paving that the SUV was initially stuck, and he had to switch the vehicle into four-wheel-drive before he was able to extricate himself and turn around.

Liang slowly retraced his route, trying to determine where he'd lost Cooper. He almost missed the tracks of Cooper's vehicle going off the road not far beyond the spot where the dust cloud ended. He followed the trail and saw that Cooper had driven off the road and doubled back. The tracks eventually turned onto a trail that led to some grazing land near the Little Missouri River.

Liang drove slowly down the trail. It was even rougher than the one they had first been on, but that wasn't the reason for his caution—he didn't want to miss any signs that might show where Cooper had turned off the main trail.

BOLAN KNEW he had problems with his vehicle before he even reached the oil-field road. The heat gauge rose beyond normal operating temperature and continued to move upward toward the red zone. The Ag Con thugs had either put a bullet through his radiator or whatever had caved in the grille had done more than cosmetic damage. Either way, the vehicle wasn't going to get them very far before its engine failed.

Kemp realized there was a problem when steam started to rise from under the hood. "Any suggestions?" she asked.

"Do you know any side trails around here?"

"Yeah, there's a trail that leads to some grazing lands along the river. One of our clients runs his cattle down there."

"Where's the turn? Point it out to me. I'm going to double back to it. That way our dust cloud will make it harder for them to see where we turned off."

"It's coming up on our right," Kemp said. "It's... here."

Bolan drove about a quarter of a mile past the turnoff, then jammed on the parking brake, sliding into a 180-degree turn. When he was facing the opposite direction, he released the brake and stabbed the accelerator to the floor, driving down the narrow path straight back into his dust cloud. When he was roughly halfway back to the turnoff, he veered off the road, crossed the shallow ditch and drove in the grass parallel to the road. Just before he reached his turnoff, he saw the other Ag Con SUV pass by on the road at what had to have been close to top speed for the vehicle. He caught only a glimpse of the driver, but it looked a lot like the man who had shot him at the Ag Con compound. Even though Bolan had seen the men in the SUV, he doubted that the Ag Con mercenaries had seen him through the thick dust cloud, but he also knew it wouldn't be long before they realized he'd doubled back.

Bolan cranked the wheel, turning onto the trail Kemp had pointed out, and floored the accelerator, but the overheating engine didn't respond very well. He could tell the engine was about to blow.

"Past this next hill on your right there's a valley that runs down to the river. Since it's not an actual marked trail, you're not supposed to drive there, but we have more important things to worry about than getting a ticket from a ranger. Pam and I rode our horses down it when we were hunting elk last fall. It's passable."

When Bolan reached the base of the hill, he cranked the wheel to the right and careened around in a four-wheeled drift and gunned what was left of the engine, which was starting to knock loudly. He followed the small valley through a stand of juniper trees. When he reached the lowland along the Little Missouri River, the engine let out a huge bang and the cab filled with blue oil smoke.

"What now?" Kemp asked.

"I'm open to suggestions," Bolan said. "But whatever we do, we have to get away from here."

"We're just across the river from our client's ranch," Kemp said. "He's old-school—he uses horses, not ATVs. He's got some good riding horses. If we can get to his barn, we can saddle up a couple of horses and ride out."

"How deep's the river here?" Bolan asked.

"Not deep. It's too shallow for swimming."

"Then lets run through the water for as far as we can," Bolan said. "That will make it harder for them to follow us." They were already in the water and heading upstream before Bolan finished the sentence. He let Kemp lead the way.

"Is your friend going to be upset when we come walking into his ranch in the middle of the night and take his horses?" Bolan asked.

"I wouldn't exactly call him a friend, but he's friendly. His name is Harry Kadrmas. He's a retired college professor. He has a doctorate in forage physiology. I guess that means he's a grass doctor. I only know him professionally, but he seemed cool."

"Is he going to shoot us?"

Kemp thought about the question. "He just might," she said. "He's cool, but he's independent-minded and I don't think he'll take kindly to someone messing with his horses in the middle of the night. But I'm sure if we talk to him he'll let us take the horses."

Bolan considered the possibility. "That's one option, I suppose, but I'm afraid bringing him into this will put him in danger. The less he knows, the safer he is."

"Then we're going to have to be pretty quiet," Kemp said. "His dog knows me, so that should help."

They'd gone nearly a mile by Bolan's estimate when Kemp left the water and climbed the west bank. "Harry's place is just on the other side of these hills," she said, and began climbing up the side of a rock formation. She'd made it to the top and Bolan was about to follow her when he caught sight of a pair of flashlights moving in their direction, one on either side of the river.

Kemp saw it, too. She looked at Bolan for guidance. He motioned for her to get down, so she took cover behind some rocks. The last thing she saw before ducking down was Bolan slinging his gun and pulling a huge knife from a sheath in his boot.

DAN GOULD WALKED into his cousin's family room and almost threw up. When he eventually regained his composure, he said, "Gordie, what on God's good green earth have you gotten yourself into here?"

"Cousin, I wish I could tell you," Gordon Gould said, "but I'd be lying if I said I knew myself. All I know is that I've got one hell of a mess on my hands."

"Now you got that mess on my hands, too. I don't know what the fuck you're into, but if it's murder, and it sure as hell looks like somebody got murdered, maybe both of these stupid fucks, then you've just made me an accessory if I don't turn you in."

"Aw, you ain't going to do that, cousin," Gould said. "You don't want the cops looking into my business any more than you want them looking into your business, and you know, cousin, your business *is* my business."

"You threatening me, Gordie?" Dan asked.

"Just stating a plain fact, cousin."

"Okay, you know I ain't going to turn you in. But just why in the hell would you expect me to help you clean up this mess?"

"Because if you do, I'll give you $100,000 cash money."

Dan didn't need to think about the offer. "So what do we need to do?"

"Near as I can figure," Gould said, "we need to dump these bodies and clean up this room." Dan looked around the room, started to wretch once again, and this time actually did throw up. "Now damn it, cousin, we ain't never going to get this place cleaned up if you keep puking on the floor."

When Dan regained control of his gag reflex, he asked, "Where do we start?"

"First off, we need to get rid of these carcasses. Let's wrap them in a tarp and throw them in the back of Jason's pickup."

"Where's the sheriff's squad car?"

"Back at the station," Gould said. "He rode here with Jason."

The men went out to Gould's barn and returned carrying a rubber-coated canvas tarp that Gould used for covering his truck box when he hauled loads of ground feed for his horses.

"Now how we going to do this?" Dan asked. "We can't carry both of them in this tarp. Jim's too damned fat."

"Let's lay the tarp in the back of Jason's pickup, then carry both of them out there. That way we won't get no blood in the box."

"What the hell difference does that make?" Dan asked.

"We won't leave any DNA evidence that way, you damned fool," Gould replied. "That way they won't be able to send any of those forensic teams like on TV after us. Plus you can take the pickup to auction and sell it."

"You think that's a good idea?" Dan asked.

"Hell, yes. Ain't nobody going to be missing Jason except me, and I sure as hell ain't going to send anyone looking for him. Besides, Jason sure as hell ain't going to need a pickup any longer." Dan had to admit that the plan made sense. Like everyone else in the region, the Gould boys hadn't been raised to be wasteful.

"We'll dump the bodies," Gould said, "then you can take the pickup to Minneapolis and get rid of it at auction. It ought to bring at least twelve grand."

"Can I keep that, too?" Dan asked.

"Don't get greedy, cousin. Tell you what—you help me clean up this mess and I'll split it with you fifty-fifty."

They spread the tarp in the box of the pickup and went in to get the bodies. Gould grabbed the sheriff by the arms, which were slippery with blood and brain matter, and Dan grabbed the feet. "Oh, my Christ!" he said when they picked up the big man's body. "He shit himself."

"I think they both did," Gould said, "or Jason pissed his pants, at least. Happens a lot."

"You spend a lot of time in close quarters with dead bodies?" Dan asked.

"I did in Vietnam," Gould said, and Dan shut up. Vietnam was a sore subject between the two of them, because Dan had got out of going because he'd drawn a high draft number. Gould suspected that Dan's old man, Phillip, had greased a few palms to get his cousin that number.

They carried the soiled, bloody bodies to the truck and placed them in the tarp. "Should we wrap them up?" Dan asked.

"No. Let's clean up the house first. Then we can throw the rags in with the bodies and bury them all together."

Gould dug out some cleaning supplies and the two men tried to scrub the blood, brains, urine and feces from the carpet and walls, but the job was so disgusting that Dan once again vomited. That was too much for Gould. He could take the rest of it, but the bourbon he'd been drinking wasn't settling well in his stomach, and for some reason the sight of Dan throwing up was more than he could handle. Moments after Dan first lost the contents of his stomach both Gould men were vomiting on the floor.

When they finally overcame their nausea, they had a bigger mess than ever to clean up. Dan looked at the mess and started weeping. That was the last straw for Gould. It was bad enough that he had to watch Dan puking on his floor, but the sight of him crying was more than he could take. He'd maybe seen two grown men cry in the forty years since he got back from Vietnam, tops, and now he'd had to endure the sight twice in the same day.

He pulled Dan up off his knees and slapped his face. Gould wasn't a big man, but he was wiry, strong and fast. Dan was big, but was soft and slow. He took a swing at Gould, but his cousin just grabbed his fist with one hand. He cocked the other and when it connected with Dan's jaw, all the man saw was blackness mixed with flashes of light. He dropped to the floor, unconscious.

"Get up and start cleaning this mess up!" Gould shouted, but his cousin was beyond hearing him. Gould was still shouting when his phone rang. It was Chen.

LIANG FOLLOWED the trail until it ended in a large pasture in the valley along the Little Missouri River. He circled the entire meadow, but the area was a boxed canyon, bordered by the river on one side and steep cliffs on the others. The only ways in or out were the trail that they'd just come down or crossing the river.

The river was shallow and had many low-water crossings where roads ran right through it, but unless there was a marked crossing, it was too risky to try to drive through unless a vehicle was equipped with water-crossing snorkels for the air intake system—and none of the Ag Con vehicles were.

That meant that Cooper and Kemp had turned off the main trail somewhere and Liang had missed their tracks. He doubled back, fighting the urge to drive quickly because he didn't want to miss signs of Cooper's trail a second time.

When they were roughly halfway back to the oil-field

road, Liang spotted what he was looking for—fresh tracks in the grass leading off the trail into a valley. He followed the tracks down to the river, where he found Cooper's vehicle, steam and blue oil smoke still rising from the engine.

"Spread out and find them!" Liang ordered. "One of you cross the water and cover both banks. I'll do the same." Liang crossed the river. He and one of his men followed it to the north, and the other two men went south.

Liang scoured the far bank while the other man scouted the near bank. They slowly made their way north, looking for any sign of Cooper and Kemp. The second pair did the same in the opposite direction. After the southbound pair had walked about a mile, the man on the west bank stopped to urinate. His partner saw what he was doing and just shook his head. Proper etiquette for males around the world was to look away from a man who was urinating outdoors. That was as true for members of the PLA as it was for soldiers in any other military organization, and the man's partner dutifully looked away while he tended to his bodily functions.

As he urinated, the man marveled at the strange topography of the region. They had stopped beside a group of rock formations of a type the man had never encountered anywhere besides this peculiar place. Smooth, rounded rocks rose perhaps fifteen feet from the riverbank like the shoulders of an elephant.

The man looked more closely at the rocks and saw footprints leading from the river toward the rocks. He was about to alert his partner when a hand covered his mouth. He felt cold steel pierce the skin of his neck and the knife blade sink into his flesh. When the blade sliced through his spinal cord, he no longer felt anything.

After what he believed to be a decent amount of time,

the man's partner finally chanced a look to see if the guy was done urinating. But his partner appeared to have disappeared without a trace. He called the man's name but only heard silence in return.

The PLA soldier waded across the river, which was waist-deep in places, and emerged at the spot where his comrade had stopped to urinate—but he saw no sign of his comrade.

Upon closer inspection he saw a spray of thicker fluid that hadn't soaked into the ground as the urine had—it was blood. The soldier followed the splashes of blood to the edge of the peculiar rock formation and saw a boot sticking out from behind a rock. It was the type of work boot that he and his comrades wore as part of their Ag Con uniforms. The man raised his gun and slowly moved toward the boot. When he got closer, he saw a pair of legs behind the rocks.

The man had heard nothing, and wasn't certain if his partner had hurt himself or if he'd been attacked, so he prepared for the latter. But he wasn't prepared for the large man who sprang up from behind the rock, driving a long knife blade up under his chin. The blade penetrated the flesh, drove through the bone that formed his brain pan and finally lodged deep within his brain stem. The man fell dead before he even realized he'd been attacked.

BOLAN WIPED OFF the seven-inch blade of his fighting knife on the dead man's shirt, folded the blade and returned it to his boot sheath. He relieved the bodies of a couple of full magazines for the QBZ, along with a drop pouch for each leg in which to carry them, then he tossed both bodies in the water and kicked dirt over the blood clotting in the dusty clay. He took a juniper branch and brushed away his tracks as best he could before climbing up to where Kemp hid in the rocks above. The subterfuge wouldn't fool an experienced tracker, but it should be enough to keep most of the Ag Con goons from finding them in the dark. And Bolan was certain that there would be more coming after them.

Kemp led the way to the Kadrmas ranch, with Bolan keeping an eye out behind them, watching for any more Ag Con men. Harry's dog barked, but it did seem to know Kemp and she was able to calm the animal before it made too much noise.

The horse barn wasn't locked, but then few people in the area ever locked doors. Everyone knew everyone else, so there wasn't much point to locking doors. Kemp took some saddles, bridles and other tack that hung from the walls of the barn and began saddling a mare. Bolan started to do the same thing with a gelding, but Kemp said, "Don't take that horse. He's useless. Harry only keeps him around because he feels sorry for him. Take that one." Kemp pointed to a stallion in the next stall.

"A stallion?"

"He's a bit spirited, but he's well-broke—more or less. Harry rides him all the time. You're a big boy. You can handle him." Bolan did as instructed. The horse seemed calm enough.

They'd just finished securing their gear and were ready to lead the horses out of the barn when the door burst open. Before they could react, Bolan and Kemp found themselves staring down both barrels of a Remington side-by-side double-barreled 12-gauge shotgun. It was so old that it still featured two exposed hammers.

"Who's in here?" Harry Kadrmas asked.

"It's me, Kristen Kemp. This is my friend Matt Cooper."

The old man lowered the shotgun and said, "Do you

mind telling me what in God's name you're doing saddling up my horses in the middle of the goddamned night?"

"Harry, they've got Pam. And Roger Grevoy."

"Who's got Pam and Rog? You're not making any sense, Kristen."

"Ag Con. They've kidnapped Rog and Pam. They're holding them prisoner at that place they bought in the Killdeer Mountains."

"Kristen, I know those Ag Con people are some crooked sons of bitches, but kidnapping? You can't be serious."

"I'm dead serious, Harry." She told him an abbreviated version of the entire story, including what she knew about the signs of prion disease that Grevoy had found, ending with their narrow escape from the Ag Con men.

"If what you're saying is true, I'm going with you," Harry said.

Bolan spoke for the first time. "I'm afraid I can't let you do that. In fact, I'd appreciate it if you could take Ms. Kemp and drive the both of you to town. Going into the Ag Con facility is going to be a borderline suicide mission. I barely made it out alive the last time I tried it. I might not be as lucky this time."

"There's no way you're getting rid of me," Kemp said. "Haven't I been useful so far?"

"You have. But the situation is going to heat up. I'm taking this war to a whole new level. I'll have a better chance if I go in alone."

"Kiss my ass," she replied. "I'm going with you."

"Me, too," Kadrmas said. "I didn't get this from shrinking from battle in Vietnam." He pointed to his leg, and for the first time Bolan realized that it was a prosthetic.

"Look," Bolan said, "I know how you feel, and I appreciate what you both have to offer, but the reality is that in an insertion operation like the one I'm planning, the two of you will just slow me down. I need to work alone on this." He looked at Kemp. "Thank you for everything you've done for me. It will mean a lot to me to know you're safe."

"Do you even know how to get where you're going?" Kadrmas asked.

"I have a good idea."

"It's about a twenty-mile drive from here to Ag Con's Killdeer Mountain facility, but that's only because you have to drive back out to the highway, then drive all the way around to the east side of the mountains to get to Gap Road. That's a long haul on horseback."

"Do you have a vehicle I can use?" Bolan asked.

"I have something better—a good idea."

"I'm listening."

"It's a twenty-mile drive, but it's no more than seven miles, as the crow flies," Kadrmas said.

"You mean along the river? You'd have to be a crow to cover that route."

"A crow or a good strong horse," Kadrmas said, patting the stallion on the rump. "Jake here has carried me over the trails that run along the river many times. Do you have a GPS with a topo map?"

Bolan took out his GPS unit and brought up the topographic map of the area. "Look here," the older man said. "See this valley? Stick to the bottom of that and it will take you within a mile of the north end of the Ag Con property line. It's tough sledding that last couple of miles into the ranch, but Jake will get you almost all the way there, and he'll get you there by sunrise."

"Are there any tricky parts of the trail I should know about?" Bolan asked.

"There's one spot where a branch of the trail goes right,

up into the mountains, and the other branch crosses the river."

"Which one should I take," Bolan asked, and Kadrmas told him which fork to take.

"What'll we do?" Kemp asked when Kadrmas had finished explaining the trail to Bolan.

"Go to Medora," Bolan said. "That's a tourist town. The Ag Con men won't look for you there. They'd attract too much attention. Get a room at the Rough Rider Motel. That's a small mom-and-pop operation. No one will be able to get in there without drawing a lot of attention to themselves. I'll contact you when all this is over and let you know when it's safe to leave."

Kemp walked over to him. "Promise?" she asked.

"Promise," Bolan said.

8

After Chen's phone call, Gordon Gould tried to awaken his unconscious cousin. "Damn it, Dan, wake up," he said, shaking the larger man. He tried slapping the man, shaking him, even dumping water on his face. Finally he kicked Dan in the testicles. It wasn't a hard, direct kick; it was more of a graze, but it did the trick. Dan let out a bloodcurdling shriek and jerked up, clutching his groin.

"What in the fuck is going on?" he shouted. "Where am I?"

"You're at my house, cousin."

"Gordon? Did you just kick me in the nuts?"

"I had to, cousin. I couldn't wake you up."

Dan rubbed his jaw and looked around at the filthy room. The events of the night started to come back to him. "You hit me!"

"Yeah, cousin, I'm sorry about that."

"Why the hell did you have to go and hit me?"

"You were bawling like a freshly weened calf," Gould said. "It was unseemly."

"Christ, Gordie, you didn't need to hit me. And you

sure as hell didn't need to kick me in the nuts. Why'd you need to wake me up so bad?"

"We got help coming."

"Help?" Dan asked. "Someone else know about this damned mess?"

"Yeah. I've got some business partners who have a vested interest in all this."

"Business partners? What the hell you talking about, Gordie?"

"I'm working with those Chinese businessmen out at Ag Con."

"Goddamn it, Gordie, what are doing hooking up with those people? They're nothing but trouble."

"You got a problem with foreigners, Dan? I never took you to be a racist."

"Hell, no. You know what my problem is, Gordie. My problem is those Ag Con bastards are nothing but a bunch of gangsters and thugs."

"How does that make them different than the North Dakota Cattle Raisers' Association? Or the oil companies or the coal companies? Or the state legislature, for that matter?"

"I'll tell you what the difference is," Dan said. "You ever have to scrape the brains of a law-enforcement officer off your wall when you were dealing with the association or the coal companies or the legislature? That's the damned difference. I'm getting the fuck out of here before those goons get here. You can keep your $100,000."

"I'm afraid I can't let you do that," Gould said. "The head of Ag Con needs you to do him a favor."

"He can go fuck himself," Dan said. "I'm out of here."

Dan got up to leave, but Gould stood in the doorway. He held a compact 1911 autoloader in his hand, cocked, but not locked. "I said I can't let you do that," Gould said. "The head guy wants you to fly him to Iowa in your plane." Dan owned a 1990 Beechcraft Baron 58, a twin-engine airplane.

"What are you going to do, Gordon, shoot me?"

"I don't know, Dan. All I know is that if you don't come through for me on this one, the Chinese could very well shoot me."

"Then put the damned gun away, Gordie. You're making me nervous." Gould flicked the safety to the "on" position and put the .45 back in his inside-the-waistband holster. "You really think that son of a bitch will kill you if I don't fly him to Iowa?"

"I know he will. I didn't realize what a badass he was until all this started."

"Just what exactly is 'all this'?" Dan asked.

"I'll be goddamned if I know, Dan. Whatever it is, it's real bad. But I think it's almost over. I think that if you fly him to Iowa, I might be home free. Will you do it?"

"You know that $100,000 you offered me?" Dan asked.

"Yeah."

"Make it $200,000."

"Goddamn it, Dan, you're killing me."

"Sounds to me like it's the Ag Con guy who's going to kill you, and I damn well know that you wouldn't get mixed up with men like that unless they were paying you a lot more than $200,000, so you'll still be money ahead. We got a deal?"

"We got a deal."

They had just shaken hands when a Chevy Tahoe filled with security guards from Ag Con pulled up. A five-man crew came in and without saying a word began cleaning up the mess from the shootings. The man who appeared to be in charge, a large, square-headed blond fellow with a strong Polish accent, said, "Where are the bodies?"

"In the back of the pickup," Gould said. "We wrapped them in a tarp."

"Good," he said. "We'll dispose of the bodies and the vehicle at the same time."

"I don't suppose we could get the pickup back when you're finished?" Gould asked.

"We'll dispose of the bodies and the vehicle at the same time," the man repeated.

"Come on," Gould said to Dan, "let's go get your plane ready and fly it to Weydahl." Weydahl Field Airport was a small airstrip just north of Killdeer, the closest landing strip to Ag Con's Killdeer Mountain facility. It was where Dan was supposed to pick up Chen. Gould planned to accompany his cousin to make sure he carried through on his end of the deal.

LIANG AND THE OTHER Chinese man walked for miles down the riverbanks without seeing any sign of Cooper and Kemp. Finally Liang decided it was time to turn around. They scoured the riverbanks just as closely on the way back to the vehicle but saw nothing of value.

Liang radioed the other two men. When he received no response, he and his partner quickened their pace. It could have been a simple radio malfunction, but given the events of the past several days, the colonel doubted it would turn out to be anything simple.

As they neared the vehicles, Liang saw something that confirmed his worst fears—the bodies of his two comrades floating in the water, headed north, downstream toward the Missouri River, or the "Big Missouri," as the locals called it in order to differentiate between it and the Little Missouri.

Liang had almost been willing to concede defeat, but

the sight of his fallen comrades told him that Cooper had to be in the vicinity.

"Keep going!" he shouted to his partner, and they continued past the vehicles, in the direction from which the bodies had floated.

The colonel almost missed the spot where the men had to have been killed. Cooper had done a fair job of covering the blood and disguising his tracks, but he had been rushed and had left a few splashes of blood on a rock. Once Liang knew that Cooper had brushed over his tracks, it was easy to discern the area that had been brushed.

It appeared as though his quarry had gone west, up the large rock formations. Liang whistled, and when he had his partner's attention he motioned that they would head west. The man crossed the river and the pair climbed the rocky riverbank.

At the top of the rocks Liang saw the likely destination for Cooper and Kemp, a small ranch nestled in the Badlands. Lights were on in the barn and the house, which was peculiar, since it was after one in the morning, and the locals tended to go to bed early. Liang caught a glimpse of taillights heading southwest along the long driveway. Cooper and Kemp were escaping.

He scanned the ranch yard for another vehicle he could commandeer in order to pursue his quarry. He settled on a flatbed truck as the most likely choice when something caught his eye off in the distance. He lifted his rifle and couldn't quite believe what he saw through the scope—Cooper disappearing into the hills on horseback. He was headed northeast, roughly in the direction of Ag Con's Killdeer Mountain facility. Though it was a fairly long drive, since they'd have to circumvent the river and the mountains, if there was a path along the river that was passable on horseback, Cooper could get to the facility in about the same amount of time as it would take Liang to return to his vehicle and drive back.

Desperate, the colonel looked for some means of pursuing Cooper. He saw that there were more horses inside the barn—one of them even appeared to be saddled and ready to ride. Liang handed his sat phone to his comrade and told him, "Call Chen. Tell him Cooper is headed toward the Killdeer Mountain facility on horseback along the river. Tell him to use every man available to secure the perimeter. Then go to the vehicle and get back to the facility as quickly as possible. Tell Chen to be prepared for war."

"What will you do?" the man asked.

"I'm going after Cooper." Liang left the man and ran toward the barn. When he reached the building he was exhausted, but adrenaline kept him moving. Inside the barn he found a mare that was saddled and ready to ride as he'd thought. It seemed odd, but he wasn't going to question his luck. He stuck his rifle in the scabbard attached to the saddle, mounted the horse and rode off in the direction he'd seen Cooper leave.

The trail was rough and it was a moonless night, but it never really got completely dark in the Badlands. With no light pollution to obscure them, the stars shone so brightly that they illuminated the landscape. When one's eyes acclimated to the light, it was possible to see clearly on the darkest nights if the sky was clear. And this night the sky was as clear as Liang had ever seen it.

The Ag Con agent pushed his horse as hard as he dared, but Cooper had a good lead on him. Even so, Liang was fairly certain he was on the right track because there weren't many alternatives to the path he followed—the rest of the area was virtually impenetrable.

At one point Liang had to make a decision between riding up into the mountains or crossing the river. Since the trail heading into the mountains seemed the most direct route to the Ag Con facility, he chose that path. It wound toward the top of the Killdeer Mountains. They were really just large hills, but because the elevation of the rest of the region was so low, they towered over the surrounding landscape.

When Liang reached the top, he realized he'd made a mistake. This trail led to the west side of the mountains. If he kept following it, it would take him all the way around to Gap Road, but that would take at least another two hours, and it most certainly wasn't the route Cooper had taken. So he rode back down and when he reached the fork in the trail, he chose the path that led to the water.

He crossed the river, which by this point had angled eastward and was flowing toward the Missouri River. The water was starting to get quite deep this close to the Big Missouri. Had the water been much deeper, his horse would have needed to swim across. He followed the trail for about two miles. Looking at the rugged terrain on the opposite side of the river made him understand why the path led along this side—the opposite side was impenetrable. Liang knew the trail would have to cross the river one more time because the upcoming terrain on this side was even more rugged, and as soon as the terrain on the opposite bank began to level off a bit the path did indeed head back into the water.

Once again the water was deep, but still not deep enough to force his horse to swim across. Once back on the other side of the river, the trail headed into the hills. This time there were no options—this was the one and only possible course. Liang rode his horse up a series of switchbacks and reached a small plateau. There he found

Cooper's horse tethered to a fallen juniper tree. The man was nowhere in sight, but Liang knew where he was heading—they were less than half a mile from the fence marking the north perimeter of the Ag Con facility.

WHEN BOLAN SAW that Kadrmas and Kemp were on their way to the relative safety of Medora, he rode off following the trail that Kadrmas had pointed out. He rode slowly at first, watching the taillights of Kadrmas's pickup disappear down the long driveway, making certain they were safe. Once they were out of sight he picked up the pace.

When he felt comfortable enough with the horse to loosen the reins, Bolan took out his sat phone and called Stony Man Farm. He gave Kurtzman an abbreviated version of everything that had happened since they'd last spoken. "I'm heading for the Killdeer Mountains compound," Bolan said. "I'm about thirty minutes out. Have you uncovered anything else?"

"Yeah," Kurtzman said. "I've got some names for you. Chen Zhen and Colonel Liang Wu. We suspect Chen is the mastermind behind the Ag Con buyout, and everything points to his being behind the plot to poison the country's beef supply with prions, as well. He's personally overseeing Ag Con's North Dakota operations. If you plan to cut off the head, he's it."

"Who is Colonel Liang Wu?" Bolan asked.

"He's the man who started the Guangzhou Military Region Special Forces Unit program."

"So basically you're telling me that I'm up against the father of China's special forces program."

"That would be him. Have you run into any particularly tenacious opponents?"

"I have," Bolan said. "The man who shot me would fit that description."

"Watch for him, Striker. He's dangerous."

"I've noticed."

"We've also uncovered the name of the man leading the research team working on the prions—Zoeng Wei. He was one of China's top genetic researchers, but he disappeared from the scientific community about two years ago. Most of his colleagues assumed he had run afoul of the Chinese government, but it turns out he's been working for the cabal that bought Ag Con all this time."

"What have you been hearing from the chatter among the local law-enforcement agencies?" Bolan asked.

"It appears that Sheriff Jim Buck has gone AWOL," Kurtzman said. "His squad car is at the sheriff's office, but there's no sign of him. Apparently his wife was arrested for prostitution at the Four Bears Casino in New Town early this morning. Most of the locals assume that's why the sheriff has disappeared. We have reason to think otherwise."

"Why's that?" Bolan asked.

"We intercepted a cell phone transmission between a couple of suspected local drug kingpins, a couple of cousins named Gordon and Dan Gould."

"I've heard of Gordon Gould," Bolan said. "He's some sort of bigwig with the local cattlemen's association. And I've seen the other one's name on damn near every used car lot in this part of the state. They're narcotics traffickers?"

"Big-time meth producers, we think. They use the auto dealerships to launder the money."

"What do they have to do with this?" Bolan asked.

"Gordon Gould is tight with Ag Con. He's on the board of trustees for their U.S. operations. He's definitely a person of interest. We intercepted a phone call between him and his cousin that mentioned a problem with the sheriff."

"Do you know where I can find these two?"

"I've got a pretty good idea," Kurtzman said. "Dan Gould is a pilot, and he flies a twin-engine Beechcraft. He just registered a flight plan a few minutes ago."

"Where's he going?" Bolan asked.

"His ultimate destination is Ames, Iowa."

"Let me guess," Bolan offered. "Ag Con has a major cattle-feed distribution operation in Ames."

"You're correct. But he's making one stop along the way, at a small airstrip north of Killdeer. It's about ten miles from the Ag Con facility in the Killdeer Mountains."

"Maybe Chen had to arrange alternate travel plans when I shot down one of his helicopters," Bolan said, thinking out loud.

"Sounds like a good possibility. It looks like they're about to put their plan into motion any moment. You don't have much time."

Bolan signed off and put away his sat phone, then gave the horse his heels. The trail was rough but Kadrmas had trained the horse well and he trotted over the rocky, steep terrain with relative ease. Bolan made it to the GPS coordinates he'd selected more quickly than he'd anticipated.

By that time the sun was coming up. He pulled his QBZ assault rifle from the scabbard attached to the saddle and made sure it had a full 30-round magazine. He stuffed his remaining magazines into one of the drop pouches strapped to his leg, took a long drink of water from the canteen he was leaving behind, and jogged off toward the perimeter of the Ag Con compound.

When he was within about one hundred yards of the fence, he spotted a patrol. Two Chinese men armed with assault rifles were walking down what appeared to be a

well-trodden path through a depression that ran between
two rocky ridges. Bolan climbed atop a ridge and waited
for them to approach.

The Executioner slung his rifle, pulled the combat
knife from its boot sheath and unfolded the blade. As the
two guards passed beneath his position, Bolan leaped forward. The tops of their heads were about five feet below
the rock from which the soldier launched himself, and his
boot heels caught one of them right on the top of his skull.
The man collapsed under his assailant's weight, and the
soldier could feel the bone in the man's skull crushing
beneath his boots when they hit the rocky ground.

The other man started to shout, but before he'd even
hit the ground Bolan had swung the knife in a wide arc,
bringing the tip of the blade straight down through the top
of the second guard's skull. All three men toppled to the
ground, but only Bolan stood up again.

The Executioner looked around to see if anyone had
heard the commotion, but the coast appeared to be clear.
He once again made his way toward the fence, prepared to
encounter more patrols. By now Chen had to have known
that Liang and his men had failed to kill him, and he had
to have suspected that the soldier's next move would be to
try to rescue Bowman and Grevoy.

Bolan could tell that the fence was electrified without
even checking, just by the grass growing along its base.
The local wildlife was savvy about electric fences; the
animals would eat the grass right up to the edge of an
electric fence but wouldn't touch it. The rotting carcass of
a mule deer fawn crumpled at the base of the fence several
yards away from Bolan's position told the soldier that this
wasn't the ordinary sort of electric fence that cattle ranchers used to give their livestock mild shocks, but rather
a deadly high-voltage unit. Most companies had ceased

using this type of fence, since to be effective, it had to be lethal, which most responsible organizations considered unsafe. Bolan doubted that would be a consideration for an organization planning to kill millions of people by poisoning the food supply.

The fence was a serious piece of equipment, fourteen feet high, with twenty-eight charged strands and twenty-eight ground strands. The unit was topped by razor wire. With enough time, Bolan could probably defeat the fence, but since time was of the essence the soldier decided to try another tactic. If there were patrols outside the fence, they had to have a way to get in and out. He'd just have to find it.

WHEN CHEN RECEIVED the call from Liang's man telling him to prepare for an attack from Cooper, his worry over the mysterious stranger was tempered somewhat by his relief that Liang was coming back to the compound. The man had been behaving in a rather erratic fashion lately, but that was uncharacteristic behavior. In all the years he had known Liang, the man had represented the consummate professional soldier. Cooper had brought out something in Liang that bordered on pride, but Chen had never encountered an opponent as tenacious and skilled as Cooper, and neither, he suspected, had Liang. Chen couldn't hold it against his comrade that the ruthless American had gotten under the man's skin.

Chen watched the men in the production room loading the product into the transportation casks through thick glass. The room was sealed shut because anyone breathing in even a granule of the product would die of encephalopathy within weeks. The only way into the working room was through an air lock that could be locked shut from the outside, should something go wrong. The men working in the sealed chamber wore nuclear-biological-chemical suits, but Chen refused to enter the chamber even while wearing an NBC suit. He had seen what happened to those unfortunate enough to ingest even microscopic particles of the infected product.

"Are your men nearly finished?" Chen asked Zoeng, who stood beside him, watching the prion-infected material being loaded through the protective glass.

"They are working as fast as humanly possible," Zoeng replied. Chen detected a bit of testiness in Zoeng's voice. Normally such insubordination would have been met with swift and terrible reprisal, but this situation was far from normal; as with Liang, Chen felt that the pressure Cooper had exerted on the entire operation made a small amount of insolence, if not excusable, at least understandable.

None of that changed the fact that Chen needed Zoeng's men to finish their task immediately. If this was the fastest speed possible, then Chen needed Zoeng's men to perform the impossible.

"I appreciate that I have given you a difficult task," Chen said to Zoeng, "but the fact remains that we will likely be under attack from Cooper very shortly."

"We must have two hundred men guarding the facility," Zoeng said. "What can one man do against such odds?"

"It depends on the man," Chen said. "Until several days ago we had well over two hundred troops at our service, but this one man has cut that number nearly by half. That should still be adequate. It seems impossible that one man can overwhelm one hundred men, but given what this one man has accomplished in a very short period of time, I don't believe we can rule out any possibilities."

"Granted we are facing a capable adversary," Zoeng said, "but that doesn't negate the fact that my men are working as fast as they can."

"Then perhaps you should don an NBC suit and go assist them."

"You cannot be serious," Zoeng said. "You are well aware of the risks of going into that room, even while wearing an NBC suit."

"The risks of not going in are far greater, I'm afraid."

"Are you threatening me?" Zoeng asked.

"Please, Zoeng, do not confuse a promise with a threat. Failure at this point would be unacceptable."

Zoeng didn't respond. He knew that Chen never said anything that he didn't mean.

"You have done a remarkable job of developing the prions," Chen said, "and please do not think this in any way disregards your contribution to our plans, but as distasteful as I find the proposition, I will see that you die a painful and horrible death if you choose to disregard my suggestion that you help your men."

Zoeng still remained silent, but he'd seen the results of Chen's handiwork on the veterinarian being held at the facility. Compared to what the man had done to her, the potential for encephalopathy seemed a minor inconvenience. He began donning an NBC suit.

BOLAN MADE HIS WAY around the fence surrounding the perimeter of the Ag Con property as quickly as he could without being discovered. The terrain was rocky and steep, but he managed to make fairly good time. He'd covered about two miles before he encountered more patrols outside the fence. Wanting to conserve his energy for the inevitable battle ahead, he chose to take cover and let the pair of Chinese guards pass unmolested. He ducked into the gap between two large boulders protruding from the hillside and hoped the sun was still low enough to keep his position hidden in the shadows.

It nearly was. The two men passed within inches of Bolan, following the path as it wound around the boulders. The Executioner thought he'd avoided confrontation, but at the last moment the rearmost of the pair glanced back over his shoulder. The man's eyes grew as round as saucers when he saw the soldier crouched less than a foot away from him.

Before he could utter a sound, Bolan swung his knife upward. It entered the man just above his hipbone. The blade sliced through his entrails and split about six inches of his sternum before being stopped by the bone. The man's guts spilled out of his cavity before he even realized he'd been stabbed and he collapsed to the ground.

The only noise produced by the encounter was the thud made by the man's weapon as it hit the ground, but it was enough to alert the other guard, who had been walking about three feet ahead of his now-deceased partner. Bolan's knife was wedged tight in the first man's sternum and when the man fell, he pulled the knife from the soldier's grasp, leaving Bolan empty-handed.

When the second man registered the threat, he raised his bullpup battle rifle to his shoulder. Before he could get the gun into position, Bolan was on top of him, knocking it from his hand. The guard fell beneath his attacker, but he rolled into his fall and brought his knee up, catching Bolan right in the groin. The Executioner spun his hips to the side and managed to avoid a blow that might have led to permanent injury. He still received enough of an impact that the pain shooting through him nearly blinded him. Rocking to the side had diminished the impact of the blow, but it had also put Bolan in an awkward position for fighting, leaving him unable to get the leverage needed to deliver a blow of his own. The sentry took advantage of that and lunged at the soldier. He grabbed Bolan's throat with both hands and once again drove a knee into the soldier's lower abdomen.

By this time Bolan had his shoulder against a rock, allowing him the leverage needed to go on the offensive. With both his hands around his adversary's neck, the guard was unable to fend off Bolan's roundhouse blow to his temple. The Executioner felt the man's grip on his neck ease off slightly, but he was still choking off the soldier's air supply, so Bolan pounded the man's head again and again, his fists driving the man ever closer to the verge of losing consciousness.

After delivering six devastating blows to the man's temple, Bolan began to fear that he would lose consciousness himself before his adversary released his death grip, but on the seventh blow Bolan felt something give beneath his fist and the man on top of him went limp.

Bolan rolled the guard off of him. Blood poured from the unconscious man's nose, eyes and ears. He wasn't dead, but most likely soon would be. If by some miracle he did survive, it would be in a comatose state.

The Executioner was starting to run low on ammunition, so he stripped several magazines from the bodies. He also discovered two Chinese fragmentation grenades on each man. These were the old-style grenades, patterned after the Soviet RGD 33 units, armed by unscrewing a wooden cap atop the grenade and pulling it loose, igniting the fuse in the process. They were crude units, but better than nothing. After Bolan confiscated the magazines and grenades from the dead sentries, he stuffed the corpses into the crevice between the rocks, hoping that it would provide better cover for the bodies than it had for him.

He continued to follow the perimeter of the fence for about another mile before coming upon an opening. It had shorter sections of chain link placed parallel with the fence, about two feet in front of and behind the opening. Two more Chinese men stood guard at the opening, but they were the only opponents Bolan could see.

The soldier crept through the sage and juniper until he'd moved into a sniping position in some rocks less than fifty feet from the opening and removed his sound-suppressed Beretta. He'd have to move with almost impossible speed if he was to drop both sentries without their firing a shot. He doubted that they'd be able to hit him in his position, but he knew that if they got off a shot, the men guarding the compound would come down on him in force. He sighted in on the head of the nearer sentry and waited until the other had turned his head to the side before he pulled the trigger.

The Beretta coughed and a single round tore through the bridge of the sentry's nose. A bloody lump of cartilage blossomed between the man's eyes and he fell dead. Before he reached the ground, Bolan had the other guard in his sights. He squeezed off another round, but the man was moving, bringing his QBZ rifle into firing position. Bolan's shot tore through the man's eye and out the side of his head.

The sentry raised his rifle to his shoulder and fired, but he fired blindly because his dominant eye had exploded and his shots ran wild. Bolan flipped the selector switch and put a 3-round burst right through the man's chest. Still the guard continued to spray the air with autofire, though Bolan couldn't tell if he was still alive or if he'd died with his finger locked around the trigger. It didn't matter because the sentry was making far too much noise.

The soldier put another 3-round burst through the back of the man's head, shredding brain stem to pulp and putting an end to his gunfire.

9

Chen considered patience one of his most valuable attributes. His patience had made it possible for him to orchestrate this plan over the course of decades without ever being discovered. It had enabled him to develop a secure network that had in turn put him in contact with such like-minded individuals as Liang and Zoeng. Superhuman patience had, in fact, been necessary every step of the way to get him this close to consummating decades of hard work, denial of worldly pleasures, sacrifice and suffering.

But finally on the verge of accomplishing all he had long dreamed of, Chen's patience had abandoned him. He keyed the microphone button on the console built into a shelf just below the observation window into the lab in which Zoeng and his men worked to fill the last of the containers with the product. "How much longer, please?" he inquired of Zoeng.

"We are nearly finished," Zoeng said into the microphone inside the lab, his voice muffled to the point of barely being audible through the helmet of the NBC suit.

"Then please finish," Chen directed.

"We are going as fast as we can," Zoeng said.

"I strongly suggest that you consider going faster," Chen said.

Knowing that he was as disposable as an empty plastic cigarette lighter at this point, Zoeng ordered his men to move faster. They picked up the pace and worked until they were nearly finished filling the final container when Zoeng's worst fears became reality. They were transferring the product into the transportation casks from the sealed, rubberized sacks used for temporary storage through flexible funnels that locked onto both the casks and the sacks with an airtight seal, but the strength of that seal required the men to secure the coupling tightly. In their haste, the final coupling hadn't been properly secured, and when the man holding the temporary storage sack stumbled, he tore the coupling loose from the sack, releasing a cloud of fine particulate into the air.

As the man staggered forward, he reached out to grab something to break his fall. That something was the mask on Zoeng's NBC helmet, which gave way, causing Zoeng to inhale a lungful of the prion-laced particulate.

Zoeng smashed his fist down on a red emergency button. Lights flashed, sirens sounded and a spray of water came down on the men inside the lab. At the same time the locks on the entrances to the air lock that separated the lab from the rest of the facility closed tight. No one was going in or out until Chen punched in the correct code, and he had no intention of doing that. Zoeng's men had loaded all but one cask onto the helicopter. As tragic as Zoeng's inevitable death would be, he had delivered enough product to become expendable.

Chen ignored the screaming and pleading coming through the intercom and walked out to the helicopter pad, where the pilot already had the engine idling. "Take off," he ordered.

After the helicopter had flown away with the product safely on board, Chen summoned the Chinese special forces operative who served as his chauffeur, along with both of his bodyguards. "Has Liang returned yet?"

"No, sir," the chauffeur told him. "We have not heard from Colonel Liang."

Chen frowned. He'd intended to have Liang accompany him to the Ag Con facility in Iowa. "Please send Mr. Tang to see me," he ordered the chauffeur, "and then bring my vehicle around and prepare to leave."

Minutes after the chauffeur had left, Tang Tsu, Liang's second in command, appeared. "I understand we have not had contact with Colonel Liang," Chen said.

"That is correct, sir," Tang said.

"You have prepared for an attack from Cooper?"

"Yes, sir. My forces, what are left of them, are patrolling the perimeter and the remaining B&B men are inside the gate, prepared to defend the facility. I don't see how it is possible for him to penetrate our defenses."

"You are aware, of course, that Cooper has performed the impossible with such regularity that he makes it look routine?" Chen asked.

"I am, sir."

"Then you will not take anything for granted? You will be relentless in exterminating the American?"

"I will, sir."

"Please see that you are," Chen ordered. "Is Mr. Yao in place in the cupola?"

"He is, sir."

"Good." Having his best sniper in position restored at least a semblance of Chen's confidence.

While Chen waited for his chauffeur, he called Gould one last time. He could not afford for the incompetent cattleman to fail, and by this point the Chinese had lost all confidence in the North Dakotan.

"Yeah?" Gould said, by way of greeting.

"Where are you?" Chen asked.

"Me and Dan are at the airport, getting his plane ready for takeoff."

"I expected you to be at the Killdeer airfield already," Chen said.

"Well, expect in one hand and shit in the other and see which one fills up first," Gould blurted out. When Chen remained silent, Gould began to get nervous. Finally he said, "Sorry about that. It's just that we have to check out the plane to make sure that Dan doesn't go and get the both of you killed."

"I see," Chen said. "By all means make certain that the plane is prepared for our flight. But also please make certain that you arrive at the airfield as soon as possible."

"No worries," Gould said. "Once we get airborne, we'll be landing in no more than ten or fifteen minutes."

Chen hung up and was still waiting for his chauffeur when he heard the first shots fired from the northern perimeter of the facility. He heard several blasts from a small-caliber full-auto rifle, followed by silence. He called his chauffeur to see what was causing the delay.

"I'm refueling the gas tank," the man said. "It was empty."

"Get over here now," Chen ordered. "You have enough gas to get me where I need to go." Minutes later the chauffeur arrived. Just as Chen and his two bodyguards were getting into the vehicle, all hell broke loose at the north end of the compound.

BOLAN DIDN'T BOTHER to hide the bodies at the entrance, though he did stop to confiscate their grenades. Again, each man had two grenades, but this time they were modern Chinese fragmentation grenades, with a pin-and-spoon activation system. He wished he had a web harness to stow his gear, but he had to make do with stuffing the grenades into one of the drop pouches. Between the magazines and the grenades, the pouches bulged to the point of almost hampering the soldier's movement.

The Executioner ran off the main path that led from the gate to what he assumed was the central facility and took cover in an outcropping overlooking the route. He knew that within moments the mercenaries guarding the facility would rush out to see why shots had been fired. In less than a minute he had that knowledge confirmed—a group of about twenty men appeared, running toward the gate, three abreast.

Bolan unleashed a stream of autofire and sawed down the three men leading the charge. The rest dived into the brush lining the path. While they sought cover, the soldier crawled to a higher position in the rocks to the left of where he'd fired his first rounds.

It proved to be a good move. Almost immediately upon hitting the dirt the soldiers fired on Bolan's original position. While they hammered the rocks below him, the Executioner crept along a small ledge until he was almost directly over the men. He stood up and sprayed an entire magazine into the group of guards in a sweeping figure-eight pattern. When his bolt locked open, he dropped behind the rocky ledge and moved to a new position, reloading his weapon on the way.

His second burst had taken a toll on the group. Bolan stole a quick glance as he sprinted toward his new position and saw that at least five bodies were not moving. But those that still moved presented a problem for the soldier. This time they'd seen him leaving his position and a stream of autofire motivated him to dive behind some large boulders. He landed elbow-first in a prickly pear cactus, driving the spines deep into the skin of his forearm. Though it was painful, Bolan had to either remain where he was or risk exposing himself to the gunfire below.

He crawled over the cactus to get to a shooting position, allowing the spines of the cactus to stab him in the chest. He gritted his teeth and plowed through the cactus with his chest, making his way to a rock formation that would provide him with cover for returning fire.

Once in place, he looked over the rock to assess the situation. The men below hadn't seen him escape and continued firing on the position in the rocks below him. Switching to single-shot, Bolan sighted in on the man closest to him, squeezed off a shot, instantly acquired another target and then managed to drop a third before the men below identified his position. Once again he was forced to duck to avoid return fire.

Bolan had run out of options for moving to a new location, and he still had at least nine men below trying to kill him. He needed help, and the grenades in his drop pouch would provide it. He pulled one of the primitive Soviet-style grenades from his drop pouch, untwisted the cap and yanked it, priming the fuse. The Soviet grenades had four-second fuses; since Bolan didn't know how long the fuse lasted on these Chinese replicas, he decided to err on the side of caution and counted off only two seconds before tossing the grenade toward the men below him.

Not waiting the full three seconds turned out to be a good move; a second after he'd tossed it, the grenade detonated, just as it landed among the enemy. Fortunately, the grenade seemed to have the same sixteen-yard kill radius as the Soviet original. After the grenade detonated, Bolan stood up and fired on the survivors below, putting rounds into anything that moved until all was still.

Bolan was certain there would be more men coming down the path; he had no idea how many, but he knew that he couldn't count on his luck holding out forever against seemingly insurmountable odds. He stood about a quarter of the way up a steep, rocky ridge on what would have been a foothill of the Killdeer Mountains. The ridge stood about two hundred feet high and separated him from the main Ag Con facility.

The path the guards had taken wound around the base of the ridge, and that would be the route that the next wave of gunners would take. Bolan decided that his best bet was to take the route less traveled: scale the ridge and attack from high ground. The soldier crawled up the near-vertical ridge, using exposed rocks for handholds and wedging his feet into the cracks eroded into the cliff face over thousands of years. The near constant beating to which he'd subjected his body over the past several days may have slowed him, but not enough so that anyone observing him would notice. Years of relentless training and exercise had turned the soldier into a high-functioning machine.

Although it wasn't obvious from below, the top of the ridge was more of a butte. The area atop the ridge was relatively flat, Bolan saw, forming a small meadow about thirty yards across at its widest point. The highest point was an outcropping at the southeastern edge of the meadow. The soldier scaled the rocks and nestled into a position that gave him an excellent view of the Ag Con facility. The central building seemed to be a large, old-style hip-roof barn. It was a massive building, and seemed to have two floors below the haymow, judging by the second row of windows placed high in the sidewalls. An anthill of activity emanated from the barn, but there seemed to be plenty going on around the other buildings, too. Vehicles moved in and out of a couple of large steel-pole-framed sheds, and a steady stream of people came and went from the farmhouse on the eastern edge of the building site.

A large group of guards was moving out of the building site toward the area in which Bolan had engaged the last group. He counted at least fifteen men, but it appeared that at least some had moved beyond Bolan's field of vision before he'd spotted them, meaning there were at least fifteen mercenaries intent on killing him located somewhere between him and Harry Kadrmas's favorite horse—and most likely more.

Bolan scanned the area through his rifle scope until he found what he was looking for—a Caucasian who appeared to be about average height. Using the man in his scope as a reference, the soldier estimated that he was just a bit over five hundred yards from the center of the compound. That was a long shot for the 5.56 mm NATO round through the short-barreled QBZ, but the two-hundred-foot drop would compensate for that distance somewhat. There appeared to be at least fifty or sixty men moving around in the compound. If the Executioner could reduce the number, it would make his entrance at least somewhat less dramatic. Since he'd already lost the element of surprise, he figured he might as well do a little sniping to try to rig the odds a bit more in his favor. If his aim was true, he'd be able to take out quite a few men before anyone below could get an accurate fix on his position, and he was well-situated to protect himself from any attacks from behind.

He estimated the bullet drop from his elevated position, calculated the wind speed and adjusted his point of aim accordingly. It would have helped for him to know the weight of the bullet and the strength of the powder charge, but Bolan had long ago learned to improvise with whatever was available. He hoped his best guess was accurate and squeezed the trigger.

LIANG HEARD the first shot just as he swung his leg down to dismount his horse. He moved as quickly as possible through the dense underbrush, but the sage and vinelike branches of the young juniper trees grabbed at his legs and slowed him. He hadn't gone far when he discovered the first pair of casualties.

Liang examined the bodies of his men. Neither appeared to have been shot. One's head had been smashed so thoroughly that Liang could not identify his features. The other one appeared to have been stabbed through the top of the head. The sight of his dead comrades increased his determination to kill Cooper.

That was when Liang heard an intense volley of rifle fire. It seemed to be coming from the passage through the fence on the northwest corner of the property, which was still a few miles from Liang's position. By now he was on a fairly well-worn path that his troops used when they patrolled outside the fence and he was able to make better time, but it still took far too long to reach the gate. Along the way he came across two more bodies. They were carefully concealed, and he would have missed them if he hadn't nearly tripped over one of them. The man he stumbled over appeared to have been beaten to death; the only blood coming from his corpse originated from the man's ears, mouth and nose. The other man suffered a much more gruesome fate—he appeared to have been completely eviscerated, and his entrails were on the ground next to his body.

He was looking at the hideous sight when he heard a grenade explode, followed by a number of single shots

being fired. After that the battle seemed to end. Liang
continued toward the gate and discovered two more of
his men dead. Although he hadn't been keeping count,
Liang knew that he was down to fewer than five of his
own troops; he was going to have to rely on the B&B
mercenaries to help him exterminate Cooper.

The scene that greeted him just inside the fence told
him that there would also be far fewer Build & Berg
mercs to aid in the task. Although it was impossible to tell
for certain because many of the bodies had been blown
to pieces by the grenade, the body count seemed high.
Worse yet, Cooper did not appear to be among the dead.

Liang broke into a run for the main building site. He'd
just rounded the base of the ridge separating him from the
building campus when he was nearly run down by a large
group of B&B mercenaries.

"Did any of you see Cooper?" he asked. He took their
silence to mean "no." "Then he must be in this area.
Spread out and search for him. There is a $10,000 bonus
for the man who brings me his body." The men fanned
out and began searching the area. They found no trace of
Cooper, and when Liang began to hear shots being fired
from the ridge above them, he knew why. He pointed
to the top of the cliff and shouted, "Up there! Get him!
Now!"

ONCE BOLAN HAD a good sense of his point of aim, he
worked fast, dropping one person after another in the
compound below. He selected the loners and strays in
order to keep his attack as low-key as possible, allowing
him to score even more kills. He'd reduced their number
by twelve before anyone below realized they were under
attack. Even after they grasped the situation, they had
no idea where to hide from the rifle fire raining down

upon them because they didn't know where the shots were coming from. The Ag Con facility housed several high-powered diesel generators used to provide electrical power for the research facility. Chen knew that the intense power requirements that the facility required to produce the prion-infected material would raise suspicion at the local power cooperative, hence, the diesel generators. The generators provided the required electrical power, but at the expense of creating an intense amount of white background noise. Normally this was a mere annoyance, but with the Executioner raining death on the compound, that annoyance had become lethal because it prevented the men from pinpointing the source of the sniper fire.

Bolan sighted his rifle on a man who had taken shelter behind a small tractor with a loader. Had the man chosen the correct side of the vehicle he would have been safe, but instead he elected to crouch on the side that faced Bolan. It was a fatal mistake.

Four men carrying identical rifles to the one Bolan was using ran from the house toward the walk-in door at the side of the barn. They moved too fast for the Executioner to get an accurate shot, but when they reached the doorway they were forced to change direction, making themselves targets. Bolan dropped the first man who attempted to enter the building, tripping the sentry immediately behind him. Before the man regained his footing, the soldier had placed a round directly through the guy's abdomen. It wasn't a clean shot, but it took the man out of play and stopped his two remaining comrades cold. They dropped to the ground, but from the angle Bolan was shooting, they still presented more than enough of a profile for him to put a round through each of them.

Bolan scanned the compound through his scope and saw that another guard had sought refuge behind the tractor. This target, however, had chosen the correct side of the vehicle. The soldier couldn't see the man's body, but he had a clear shot at his legs beneath the tractor's undercarriage. The Executioner put a round through his left thigh, dropping the man into view. A bullet to the top of his head ended the man's life.

Another sentry crouched behind a large aboveground diesel tank. Bolan could only see the man's knee, calf and ankle sticking out from behind the tank, but it was enough. He squeezed off a shot and the knee exploded. The man threw himself backward, pulling the tattered remains of his leg with him. Bolan was unable to get a second shot before the guy disappeared, but the copious amounts of blood that sprayed the surrounding area told the Executioner a second shot would not be needed.

A smaller aboveground tank likely housed gasoline, because when Bolan had started shooting he'd noticed a man filling a Chevrolet Tahoe from it. Since diesel-powered Tahoes were nonexistent in the U.S. market, Bolan guessed the tank contained gasoline. The man filling the Chevy SUV had been one of Bolan's first targets. He'd been holding the nozzle for the fuel pump when the Executioner dropped him, and in his death throes he had to have squeezed the handle and locked it open. His body was now surrounded with a large pool of gasoline.

Several men hid behind the tank. Bolan could see bits and pieces of their clothing, but he couldn't make out enough to get a good shot at them. But he could get off a shot at the growing pool of gasoline. Bolan fired a round, and the bullet generated a spark when it hit the rocky soil. That spark set off the pool of gasoline like a bomb. But that initial explosion was a mere trifle compared to what happened when the flames followed the hose to the pump and the gasoline tank itself. The entire compound was enveloped in a massive fireball. Bolan felt a hot wind wash over his position, more than a quarter mile away.

The explosion of the gas tank was followed by several other smaller explosions. Three SUVs were waiting to be refueled, and when the pool of gas ignited, all three of them went up in flames. The subsequent explosions had been caused by the SUVs' gas tanks erupting.

When the thick cloud of black smoke let up, Bolan couldn't see anything moving in the compound, so he started scanning the windows of the buildings. Through an upstairs window of the house, he could see a man holding a rifle scanning the hillside. Since Bolan saw him first, the soldier got off the first shot. He'd adjusted the angle of the shot to compensate for the spalling that would occur when the bullet passed through the window glass. His adjustment had to have been accurate because he saw the man lurch backward. He fell to the floor and didn't move.

Bolan was just about to sight in on another man he saw through the large open door into the upstairs haymow when he heard a booming report. At the same instant, a large chunk of rock just inches from his head burst apart. Shards of stone lacerated the soldier's face and he started to bleed, but the injuries were superficial and his eyes seemed to have been spared.

The Executioner ducked and quit firing. Remembering the last time he'd engaged an Ag Con compound, he had a pretty fair idea where to find the sniper firing the large caliber rifle—the cupola atop the barn. Bolan cut a branch from a scruffy, stunted juniper tree and carefully placed it at the outer edge of the rock he was hiding behind. Then he did the same with another branch. He repeated the process until he'd constructed an artificial bush. So far there had been no further large-caliber rifle fire, but that just meant he was facing a professional sniper and he was waiting until he got a clear shot rather than spraying him with random fire.

YAO RUI CURSED himself for taking the shot at Cooper. He knew full well that the reason he'd failed to hit his target was his own wounded pride. He had lost face when he had missed Cooper at the Trotters facility, and he had been so anxious to redeem himself that he had become impatient. When he'd seen the top of Cooper's head through his scope, he knew he didn't have enough of a target to get off a kill shot. He'd waited as long as he could stand to wait. He'd waited while Cooper shot his comrades and caused the gasoline tanks in the compound to explode. But when Cooper started firing on the occupants of the farmhouse, he could wait no longer. He convinced himself that he had a kill shot and he'd squeezed the trigger on his M98.

And he'd missed. Again. He tried to contact his partner on his radio, but he feared his fellow sharpshooter had been Cooper's target in the house. Yao could see no other movement in the compound. Other than the B&B mercenaries who had left to go aid their comrades on the north end of the property, Yao appeared to be the lone surviving defender. He knew that there likely remained the laboratory workers deep in the basement beneath the barn, and probably several administrative workers cowered somewhere in the house, but not one of those men had ever held a weapon of any type. They would be of no use.

That meant that everything rested on Yao's shoulders. That pressure made him even more remorseful about letting his own hubris prevent him from waiting for a kill shot before he attempted to take out Cooper.

Yao scanned the rocks, looking for any sign of movement. There didn't appear to be any possible way for

Cooper to escape from his position without putting himself in Yao's line of fire. All he had to do was wait. Cooper would either make a fatal mistake and expose himself in Yao's rifle scope, or the B&B troops would catch on to the man's location and attack him from the north.

At one point Yao noticed a bush that he hadn't remembered seeing before, at the bottom right-hand side of the pile of rocks behind which he had Cooper pinned. He studied the bush, but once he'd identified it as a natural feature of the terrain, he stopped focusing on it and resumed his search for some sign of Cooper.

When he once again looked at the bush, it appeared to have grown. He studied the bush again and something did not appear right. It took a few moments, but he finally realized that there was something in the bush. Gradually his eyes made out the shape of a gun barrel. Before he could react and squeeze his trigger, he saw the gun barrel in the shrub flare up. It was the last thing Yao saw before the bullet tore through his forehead.

AFTER BOLAN KILLED the sniper in the cupola, he returned to his position and scanned the area for survivors. He determined that anyone still alive was most likely a noncombatant. He was about to move down to extract Bowman and Grevoy when he heard a sound coming from north of his position.

Bolan barely had time to aim his rifle in the direction of the noise when the first opponent appeared atop the ridge. The soldier quickly registered the fact that this man had European rather than Asiatic features before he fired upon him, knocking the man back down the hill.

The Executioner's shot was met with return fire from multiple positions. Apparently the men who had gone to aid their dead comrades had decided to scale the cliff themselves and attack him from the rear. Bolan couldn't blame them—it's what he would have done himself.

Though he was outnumbered, Bolan enjoyed an advantageous position. He could hold the enemy off as long as they didn't skirt the edge of the butte and attack him on two fronts. He saw the top of a head poke up from behind the cliff and managed to get a shot off at it before it popped back down. He was rewarded for his efforts by the sight of a hunk of hair, bone and brains exploding backward.

Bolan noted that much of the fire coming his way was clustered around one particular area. He was unable to locate a target through his scope, but the area was only twenty yards away. The soldier unscrewed the cap on another of the Soviet-style grenades, yanked the fuse, counted off two seconds and hurled the bomb. Though it was a crude and antiquated device, the sticklike shape of the grenade made it ideal for throwing long distances. It spun through the air like a well-balanced knife and dropped below the horizon just about where the cluster of gunfire was most intense.

The Executioner had no idea how many opponents he'd taken out with the grenade, but he saw multiple body parts raining through the air, and after the dust settled the gunfire coming his direction was much more sporadic.

Bolan knew he could hold off the remaining men from his position, but he also knew he couldn't rescue Bowman and Grevoy while he was pinned down in a standoff situation. He decided to make a run for it. He identified at least six positions from which he was receiving fire and in rapid succession he lobbed his remaining replica grenades along with the four 86P grenades at each of those positions. The blood-curdling screams that came from his opponents let him know that at least some of them had been taken out of the fight. Judging from the lack of return fire, it seemed possible that he'd eliminated all of them. Though he received no more fire, he sprayed the opposite side of the butte with harassing fire, then leaped over the rocks and began scrambling down the side of the cliff.

He'd only made it a few steps when a man lunged at him, knocking him off his feet. Bolan and his assailant tumbled twenty feet down the side of the hill, their arms locked around each other, trying to gain the upper hand. Bolan recognized the features of his attacker—he was the same man who had shot the soldier as he'd fled the Trotters facility on horseback. It was Liang.

Bolan was much larger than the colonel, but Liang proved to be an excellent fighter. He managed to position his body so that it stopped rolling, while at the same time hurling Bolan over him and down the hill. When the big American landed, his right shoulder struck a sharp rock, breaking open the stitches and sealant over his bullet wound. He could feel blood running down his shoulder. He only hoped that the wound had healed enough by now so that he wouldn't lose too much blood and be able to keep functioning.

Liang dived down the hill after Bolan, a knife in his right hand. The Executioner thrust up his left arm and caught his adversary's wrist. At the same time he kicked upward with all the strength he had. This time Liang went hurtling down the side of the hill. The area on this side of the butte was much less steep than on the side Bolan had ascended, but Bolan had thrown his opponent with tremendous force, and Liang tumbled nearly to the base of the compound before he came to a stop.

The colonel remained still at the base of the hill, most likely unconscious, but Bolan wasn't going to take any chances with the tenacious and deadly man. He raised his battle rifle and was about to make certain that Liang's stillness became a permanent situation when he found himself being fired upon from above.

Cover was much harder to come by on this side of the ridge, and the only thing near Bolan was a small boulder, about the size of a large dog. He dived for the minimal safety the rock provided and returned fire at the top of the hill. Two men stood at the edge of the butte, and through his scope he could see that both men were wounded and bleeding profusely. He couldn't see anyone else. The men fired down at him, but they appeared shaky and their shots went wild.

Bolan wasn't in much better condition himself with the reopened wound in his shoulder, but he was used to fighting through pain, and his shots were much better placed. He dropped both men with a 3-round burst to each of them.

After he'd scanned the top of the hill to make certain no one else was coming at him from that quarter, the Executioner turned back to finish off Liang, only to find that he was gone.

10

Chen's SUV had just turned onto the main highway when he heard the explosions from the direction of the Ag Con facility. It looked like he had finished his work there just in time. It seemed impossible that a single person could wreak such havoc on a facility that well-protected. But apparently Cooper was something more than an average single person. Chen felt fortunate to have escaped from such a force without having his plans thwarted. Certainly the scope of what he was planning had been diminished, but only slightly. With the amount of product making its way to the Iowa feed-processing facility, he could be sure that the loss of life would number in the millions.

The American financial system, indeed, the entire American social fabric, was so weak that the slightest crisis could topple the entire structure, and Chen was preparing to unleash a disaster of epic proportion.

With the United States out of the way, China could assume its rightful place as the world's only remaining superpower. Currently the United States enjoyed hegemony in the world's energy market, and all other countries were forced to play by the rules the U.S. set. Once the United States were no longer united states, China could dictate the rules of the game. And Chen would see to it that the game was governed by socialist rules, not capitalist rules. Not only would the glory of Communist China be restored, but it would be elevated to undreamed of heights.

The excitement of almost achieving what he'd worked for all these years nearly overwhelmed Chen, but he knew it was too early to engage in self-congratulation. He still had to get both himself and the product to the Iowa feed-processing facility. The fact that the Gould cousins were not waiting at the Weydahl Field Airport north of the small town of Killdeer drove home the fact that his plan would not be a success until prion-infected meat entered the food supply.

Chen scanned the sky, looking for signs of the twin-engine Beechcraft, but saw nothing. He dialed Gordon Gould's number on his sat phone. "Where are you?" Chen demanded.

"We're still at the Watford City Airport," Gould said.

"And why is that?" Chen asked.

"We're waiting to fuel up the plane."

"There is a long line for refueling at an airport that size?"

"No," Gould said.

"Then what is the problem?"

"They're filling the underground tanks, and we have to wait until the tanker truck finishes before they'll turn on the pumps."

"This is unacceptable," Chen said.

"Well, what in the Sam Hill do you expect us to do about it?" Gould asked. "If we make a scene, it's going to draw attention. Given that I had two dead bodies in my recreation room, one of whom was a law-enforcement agent, I don't expect drawing attention to ourselves is a particularly good idea right now."

"Fair enough," Chen replied. "How long do you think it will take for them to turn on the pumps?"

"However goddamned long it takes, I suppose." Gould had lost patience with the demanding Chinese and no longer cared about what repercussions his insubordination might have. He just wanted to get the miserable son of a bitch out of his life once and for all. "We'll get there when we get there."

LIANG WAS RUNNING for cover before he'd even fully regained consciousness, moving on pure instinct. While he ran, he formulated a plan that became clearer as he shook off the blow to the head he had received on his tumble down the side of the hill.

Cooper was coming into the compound with one purpose—rescue the veterinarian and the county extension agent being held captive at the facility. Even if Cooper knew about the prion production taking place, the B&B men Liang had encountered on the other side of the butte had told him that Chen had loaded the product aboard the remaining helicopter. If that was true, then Chen himself had most likely escaped from the facility.

Liang had every intention of doing likewise, and he realized that the best way to get past Cooper was to use the two prisoners as hostages. The colonel made his way to the barn where the prisoners were being held and entered the lift that led to the lower levels. He leaped off the lift platform even before it hit the stops embedded in the concrete below. He grabbed the keys for the cell from the cabinet in which they were kept, along with two pairs of wrist restraints. He opened the cell door, walked in and hit the extension agent in the back of the head with his rifle butt, knocking the man to the floor, dazed, but conscious. Before the woman could react, Liang had twisted her arms behind her back and placed her wrists in the restraints.

The man was trying to get up, but Liang hit him again with the butt of his rifle, knocking him back down. The colonel rolled him over and put the second pair of restraints on his wrists.

"Get up!" he shouted at the man, raising his rifle as if to hit him again. A third blow proved unnecessary. Grevoy struggled to his feet.

"Move," Liang ordered, motioning toward the door with his rifle. "Now!"

The prisoners did as they were told. Liang motioned for them to walk toward the lift. Once they'd entered the cage, he pushed the lever to go up, but instead of stopping at the main floor, he kept going all the way up to the cupola they used as a guard post.

"Down on the floor!" Liang ordered once they'd arrived in the oversize cupola. This was a particularly unpleasant task, given that most of the floor's surface area was covered with Yao's nearly headless body, and both Bowman and Grevoy hesitated. Again Liang raised his rifle butt, but this time he brought it down between the woman's shoulder blades, knocking her to the floor. He aimed the barrel at the man and said, "Down! Now!" This time the man complied.

The colonel took the binoculars from a small shelf built below the observation window and peered out the window, looking for Cooper, but the big man was nowhere to be seen. Once again he ordered his captives to move, and this time they were quick to comply. The pair rose from the floor covered in blood.

Liang lowered the lift to the haymow level, managing

to stop it just about level with the floor. "Move!" he once again ordered his hostages, pointing toward the rear of the building where a rickety wooden staircase descended to the back of the main barn. They'd been using the area at the back as a garage, and Liang knew that this was where he had the best chance of finding a vehicle that hadn't been destroyed during Cooper's onslaught.

BOLAN SCANNED the Ag Con facility for signs of Liang and caught just a glimpse of him as he disappeared into the barn. The soldier ran toward the building, slinging the rifle and pulling his Beretta from shoulder leather; he preferred to use the compact machine pistol in close quarters. Once inside he found all manner of weaponry, including a rocket propelled grenade launcher and several cases of grenades, but he couldn't find a trace of Liang. He checked out the RPGs. They were Chinese Type 69 units that fired 85 mm grenades. He made a note of their location, thinking they might come in handy later. Just as he was about to leave and search another building, he heard an electric motor start to whir somewhere above him.

Bolan traced the sound to the area just behind a wooden staircase that led up to the haymow. He heard something moving right behind him and saw a door that looked as though it led to a storage compartment behind the staircase. He opened it and saw a pair of ropes working along rails that ran down into what looked like several layers of bunkers below the barn. He looked up and saw several people through the bottom of a steel-grate platform that was moving down from the top of the building. The lift stopped at the haymow level and the people got off the platform.

The soldier rushed up the staircase and found himself

in a dormitory area on the second floor. Rows of bunks spread across the floor, and storage lockers lined one wall. A large, open double door led to what looked like a bathroom and shower facility. He didn't see any other people, nor did he see a staircase leading to the haymow area.

A scan of the space revealed a door at the back of the large dormitory room. When he strode forward and turned the knob, he found it locked. Bolan gave it a test kick, surmised that it wasn't reinforced and kicked the door down with ease. Behind the door he found a makeshift kitchen area. In the rear of the space, which appeared to be used for storage, he found what he was looking for—a staircase leading up to the haymow. The stairs appeared to have seen little if any use for a long time, and the wood looked rotten. Bolan tested the first step and it held his weight, but just barely. He'd have to step gingerly to make it up the stairs without falling through.

He'd just made it to the third step when Liang, Grevoy and Bowman appeared at the top of the stairs. Bolan raised his Beretta, but Liang was using Grevoy and Bowman for cover. In the dim light Bolan couldn't get a clean shot at him.

"Drop your weapon," Liang ordered. "Drop it or I will shoot the man."

Bolan could see that Liang had the barrel of his bullpup rifle pressed between Grevoy's shoulder blades.

"Stay calm," he said. "No one needs to get hurt here." He raised his hands as if to drop the pistol, but he held on to it. Instead, the soldier slowly moved backward, hoping to get a better angle for a clear shot at the Chinese man.

"I said drop your weapon!" Liang shouted, pushing Grevoy ahead with the barrel of his rifle. The extension agent stumbled and lurched forward onto the top step of the staircase. Grevoy was a large man, and when he trod on the top step it gave way. He crashed through the staircase and plunged toward the floor, landing on several cartons of what appeared to be foam cups, judging from the flurry of shattered foam that cascaded through the air upon Grevoy's impact.

With the hostage out of the way Bolan had a clear shot at Liang and he took it, pumping four single rounds into the man's chest, right below the base of his throat. Each round that struck him knocked the man back several inches, but still Liang remained upright, even though blood sprayed like a geyser from his wounds.

Bolan kept shooting, walking his shots upward. He shot Liang in the throat, in the chin and in the mouth. Each shot made the man take another step back, but still he did not go down. Liang's lower mandible had been shattered by a bullet, and the round through his mouth had shattered Liang's teeth before passing through his brain pan. The man had to be technically dead, but still he remained standing. Finally Liang's body stood motionless for a moment and then slowly toppled forward.

The Executioner stared at the gruesome sight, as did Pam Bowman, who had yet to say a word. Bolan's meditation on the situation was broken by Grevoy struggling to extricate himself from the pile of cardboard and foam in which he was embedded. The soldier went over and helped him stand up.

"Are you all right?" Bolan asked.

"Yeah, I think so. Who are you?"

"Justice Department." Bolan helped the big man free himself from the foam mess he'd fallen into. When Grevoy was free, he and Bolan helped Bowman down from the haymow. Judging from her injuries, the woman had been tortured, just as Bolan had suspected. It looked like most of her injuries wouldn't leave permanent scars, but he knew from hard experience that some wounds would never heal, and those she'd have to carry with her for the rest of her life. Bowman remained silent while they helped her down.

"Do either of you know where the research facility is?" Bolan asked.

"There appeared to be a laboratory complex on the floor above where we were being held," Grevoy said.

"Do you have any idea what they were doing there?" Bolan asked.

"I have my suspicions," Grevoy said. "I think it had something to do with prions. I saw what appeared to be an air lock and several NBC suits hanging beside it."

"Yeah, that's what we think, too. Your samples came back positive. How do we get down there?"

"We'll have to take the lift that we were just on."

"'We' won't be taking anything," Bolan told Grevoy. "I want you to take Ms. Bowman and get as far away from here as possible."

"Where will we go?" Grevoy asked. "Ag Con has men everywhere around here."

Bolan suspected that might no longer be the case, given the sheer number of men he had disposed of since he arrived in western North Dakota, but Grevoy had a point. There was no sense taking chances.

"Go to the Rough Rider Motel in Medora," he told Grevoy. "Kristen Kemp and Harry Kadrmas are there. Hook up with them and make certain that Ms. Bowman is all right."

ZOENG AND HIS TECHNICIANS waited to die in the laboratory. For Zoeng it no longer mattered that they would eventually run out of air in the sealed room, since he would soon die anyway, but the remaining men held on to the hope of somehow escaping from what would otherwise become their tomb.

When they saw a man enter the outer room, they experienced a glimmer of hope that they might yet survive the ordeal.

Bolan looked around the room and realized that the men behind the window were trapped inside what appeared to be a sealed room, judging from the elaborate anteroom that served as an air lock. All the men wore yellow NBC suits, but one man had removed his mask and helmet. The rest of them appeared to not want to stand too close to the man without the helmet. Bolan looked at the console in a panel mounted below the thick glass window looking into the lab. Though the controls were all marked with Chinese characters, one button by a speaker and recessed microphone appeared to be the controls of an intercom.

The man without the helmet came up to the window and pressed a similar button on the panel on his side of the glass.

"Please," the man said over the intercom in carefully studied English, "you must let us out of here."

"Is the lab infected?" Bolan asked.

"It was," the man replied, "but it has been sprayed clean. Any remaining traces of the prion material will be removed when we are sprayed clean in the air lock."

"Are you infected?"

"I am. My associates are not. Do not worry. You will not become infected unless you are a cannibal—at this point you would have to ingest portions of my central nervous system to become infected. Please, let us out."

"How would I do that?" Bolan asked. Zoeng gave Bolan the code to punch in to unlock the air lock doors. Once the first door opened, the men in the lab moved into the air lock where they were sprayed down once again. When the disinfectant solution spray ended, the men removed their NBC suits and exited from the air lock.

When the men came out, they found themselves face-to-face with the business end of Bolan's Beretta.

"Listen closely," he said. "I didn't let you out because I'm a great humanitarian. I let you out because I need some information."

"What do you wish to know?"

"What were you doing with the prions?"

Zoeng told the soldier everything he knew about the plan, up to loading the stainless-steel casks with infected material and placing them aboard the helicopter.

"Where was the helicopter taking the infected material?" Bolan asked.

"To the Agricultural Conglomerate feed-grinding facility in Ames, Iowa."

Bolan knew that the Bell 210 would have to refuel at least twice along the way. "Do you know where the refueling stops are?" he asked.

"Mandan, North Dakota and Sioux Falls, South Dakota."

"Is Chen aboard the helicopter?"

"No," Zoeng said.

"Where is he?"

"He's procuring a private plane at the airport north of Killdeer. He's probably just arriving there as we speak."

"One last question," Bolan said.

"Yes?"

"What am I supposed to do with you?"

"I'm a dead man," Zoeng said. "I have been infected with the prions. Please, I have given you all the information I have. In return, I ask only one favor."

"What?" Bolan asked.

"Shoot me."

"I can't do that," Bolan said.

With a loud cry Zoeng charged at Bolan, holding out some sort of syringe aimed straight at the soldier's chest.

The Executioner raised his Beretta and granted Zoeng's final wish. He looked around at the other technicians. Each man possessed the knowledge to unleash the deaths of millions of people. Bolan wasn't in the business of slaughtering unarmed opponents, but he wasn't in the business of taking prisoners, either. "Do any more of you require my services?" he asked.

BOLAN DROVE the black SUV as fast as he could and still keep it on the road. He'd wasted valuable minutes locking the technicians in the cells below the lab. As soon as he got off the loose, sandy gravel road and turned onto the main highway, the soldier pulled out his sat phone and called the Farm.

"What's happening, Striker?" Kurtzman asked.

"I need you to track a helicopter that left the Ag Con facility within the past hour," Bolan replied.

"You want us to shoot it down?"

"Not a good idea," Bolan replied. "It's loaded with what amounts to prions in concentrated powder form. Shoot the helicopter down, and anyone downwind of the crash site will be dead within weeks. Just find it and let me know where it is. I'll figure something out."

"Of that I have no doubt," Kurtzman said. "What about the facility?"

"Sanitize it," Bolan said, "with extreme prejudice."

"Did you leave any survivors?"

"A few lab techs locked up in the lowest level of the barn. You'll want to bring them in for interrogation. I suspect that there's much we can learn from them."

"After that?" Kurtzman asked.

"Burn the place to the ground. Same goes for the Trotters facility."

While he'd been talking to Kurtzman, Bolan had kept the throttle on the big V-8 engine pinned. Normally the trip would have taken half an hour, at least, but Bolan made it to the airport in less than twenty minutes. Calling Weydahl Field an airport would have been an exercise in flattery; the entire facility consisted of a long, narrow concrete runway with a small metal shed on the south end that served as a hangar. The only vehicle present was an Ag Con truck, twin to the one that Bolan drove.

A twin-engine Beechcraft that matched the description that Kurtzman had given him of Gould's plane was just touching down on the runway when Bolan neared the airport. Bolan kept the accelerator pinned to the floor until he was almost about alongside the steel building and then stabbed the emergency brake pedal just as the Beechcraft taxied up to the building. The rear wheels of the large SUV locked and the vehicle spun so that it was facing the opposite direction by the time it came to a halt. Bolan couldn't see any people inside the other SUV because of the dark tinted windows, but he wasn't about to take any chances. He grabbed the RPG he'd liberated from the barn, maneuvered it out the driver's window and fired a round into the Ag Con vehicle.

Once the truck erupted in flames, lighting up the interior, Bolan could see a man sitting in the driver's seat, trying desperately to escape. He opened the door and burst out, but he was already enveloped in flames. The man threw himself on the ground and rolled around, trying to extinguish the fire, but soon quit moving.

Suddenly gunfire erupted from inside the building. The shots coming through a walk-in door set in the side of the building struck the front of Bolan's vehicle, smashing out the glass lenses of the headlights. The building was just a pole-type shed, constructed of thin corrugated steel tacked to a framework made of wooden poles. The soldier's vehicle didn't offer him the best protection, but it was better than the protection afforded the men inside the shed. He estimated the location of the shooters from the angle through which the shots came out of the building, grabbed the QBZ rifle sitting beside him on the seat, and emptied a 30-round magazine into the walls. His rounds stitched holes through the corrugated steel at waist level. When no return fire came back from the building, Bolan loaded another grenade into the RPG launcher and fired into the structure. The grenade detonated on impact and created a ten-foot hole.

Bolan could see two bodies lying in the twisted metal wreckage, both wearing the tattered remains of the de facto Ag Con uniform—khaki trousers and blue denim button-down shirts. He spotted nothing moving in the interior of the building. He'd almost decided that the area had been cleared of bad guys when someone opened up with automatic rifle fire.

The man shooting at Bolan was on the far side of the building. Though he didn't have a clear shot at the soldier through the hole left by the RPG round, some of his shots were coming dangerously close, hitting the front fender of the SUV. Bolan slammed the accelerator to the floorboards, drove down through the ditch and up the other side, catching air. He crashed through a fence before his wheels once again touched down and almost lost control, but managed to keep the vehicle pointed more or less at the hangar. While he drove, he pulled his Beretta from its holster and fired into the building. He skidded to a stop just outside the large overhead door that opened into the interior of the hangar. The man remaining inside the building continued to fire at him, but now Bolan could see why his aim was off—half the man's face had been blown away by shrapnel from the RPG. Bolan recognized the half of the face that remained from images that Kurtz-man had sent him—it was Chen. Bolan finished off the man with a 3-round burst that obliterated most of what remained of his face.

While Bolan was doing this, the plane had reversed direction and was taxiing back to the runway. The soldier slammed the Tahoe into gear and accelerated toward the airplane. He passed it on the dirt alongside the runway, cranked the wheel and skid sideways to a stop, right in front of the aircraft.

The plane skidded to a stop. A man Bolan hadn't seen before jumped out the side door onto the wing and aimed a 1911-style pistol at him. The man was behind the large propeller of the twin-engine plane; the rotation of the pro-peller and vibration on the wing threw off his aim and his shots went high.

Bolan found himself under no such constraints. He raised his Beretta and put a 3-round burst into the man's shoulder, which was the only part of his body exposed behind the spinning propeller. The man tumbled back-ward and fell off the wing, but he still held on to the pistol. He rolled into a prone position and fired at Bolan, hitting the door frame just inches from the soldier's head. Bolan switched his Beretta to full-auto and unloaded the rest of the magazine into the man, stitching him from the back of his head down his spine. Bolan dropped the empty Beretta and pulled out his Desert Eagle, putting the pilot square in his sights. He intended to fire at him, but the man appeared to be unarmed. The soldier jumped from his vehicle, ran to the plane and shouted, "Get out!"

The man throttled down the plane and exited the cockpit. When he came out, Bolan could see that he'd voided his bladder. "Don't hurt me!" the man screamed.

Bolan frisked the man and found that he was unarmed. "Are you Dan Gould?" Bolan asked.

"Yes."

"You and I are going to identify some bodies back in the hangar," Bolan said. "Then we're going for a ride in your airplane."

As SOON AS Bolan and Dan Gould were airborne, the soldier contacted Stony Man Farm to learn the location of the helicopter carrying the prion-infected material. They were too late to catch the helicopter at its refueling at the Mandan Airport, but Dan's plane was much faster than the converted Huey and they were able to get to the Sioux Falls Regional Airport before the helicopter.

When they landed, Bolan made Dan sit in the rearmost seat and secured his hands to the brackets attaching the seat to the floor of the cabin with plastic zip ties. At first Dan had appeared to have been in a state of shock and Bolan worried about his ability to fly the plane, but once they were airborne Bolan realized the man was simply in a state of near-paralysis from fear. That fear made Dan easy to manipulate, and Bolan doubted he would try to make a break for it. But until the helicopter and its toxic contents were neutralized, the stakes were too high for the soldier to leave anything to chance.

Bolan looked his terrified pilot straight in the eye and asked, "Do you have any doubt that I will kill you if you cause me the slightest bit of trouble?"

Dan looked like he was trying to answer, but all that came out of his mouth was a loud sob, so he answered Bolan's question by shaking his head.

"Do as you're told, and you might live through this," Bolan said. "Disobey me in the slightest, and I will kill you. Frankly, I don't give a damn either way. The choice is yours. Do you understand me?"

Dan answered by nodding.

Once the pilot was secured, Bolan called Stony Man Farm. "Bear, do you have an ETA on that Bell?" he asked.

"You've got approximately seventeen minutes to prepare, Striker," Kurtzman said. "The refueling facility is at the northeast corner of the airport. We've got a hazmat team en route to the airport, but it won't arrive in time. It's up to you to secure the package alone. We've contacted the head of airport security, and he should be meeting you any minute."

"Do we have a plan?" Bolan asked. "This is a fairly busy airport. If I go in cowboy style with guns blazing, there's a strong potential for collateral damage."

"The security chief is bringing you a pair of coveralls identical to those the staff at the refueling station wears," Kurtzman said. "You're going to handle the refueling of the helicopter. I don't think you need me to tell you how to take it from there."

"Here's the security chief now," Bolan said. "I'll check back in when I've taken control of the helicopter."

Bolan exited the plane and met the man bringing him the blue cotton coveralls. The name tag over the breast pocket read "Jerry." The soldier shed his shirt and trousers and donned the dark blue cotton jumpsuit, then made his way over to the refueling facility, arriving just as the helicopter set down.

The Executioner didn't need to tell the other workers to lay low; the head of security had to have briefed them and they were all beating a hasty exit from the area when

Bolan arrived. He also had no cause to interact with the pilot, who had radioed ahead with his fuel order, so the soldier went straight to the fuel pump and began rolling out enough hose to reach the helicopter. He began to fill the Bell's tanks, which would take a while, since they held a total of nearly three hundred gallons.

While the first tank filled, Bolan casually walked around the helicopter, as if checking it over. When he was beside the pilot, he took a pen out of the breast pocket and reached into his coveralls, as if pulling out a clipboard. Instead, he'd planned to pull out his .44 Magnum Desert Eagle, but just as he reached into the coveralls, the pilot pulled up a QBZ Type 97B rifle, a short-barreled compact version of the Type 97 designed for close-quarters combat and use in vehicles. The pilot had to have recognized Bolan as Cooper, even though he was sure he'd never seen the man before. Chen had to have made certain everyone at the Ag Con facilities had memorized his face. Even though Bolan had tried to be as careful as possible, he supposed that he'd been caught on a security camera at some point.

When Bolan saw the barrel of the gun come up, he dived for cover under the helicopter. The pilot fired through the Plexiglas side window, but the soldier was under the helicopter before the pilot squeezed the trigger. Bolan heard the engine of the helicopter turn over and knew he was running out of time. He moved just underneath the foot well of the helicopter, which was covered with brown-tinted Plexiglas, and fired a round up into the cabin. The .44 Magnum round hit the pilot's foot with enough force to disintegrate it from the ankle forward.

In spite of his agony, the pilot swung his rifle around and emptied an entire magazine through the window, just missing Bolan as the soldier ducked back down under the helicopter. Being a refurbished military Huey, the Bell 210 had underbelly armor that couldn't be penetrated by 5.56 mm NATO rounds, so once under the aircraft, Bolan was out of reach of the pilot's bullets.

The Executioner heard the engine power up and the helicopter started to lift into the air. The soldier lunged up, pulling himself onto the skid, thrust his Desert Eagle through the shattered Plexiglas covering the side window and emptied the remaining magazine into the pilot, shredding the man from just below his armpit to the top of his head.

The dead pilot lurched forward, and when he did, the entire helicopter slammed down into the ground nose-first. Bolan managed to maintain his grip on the window frame when the helicopter fell the two feet it had risen, but the engine was still running at full throttle. The helicopter skidded ahead on its nose toward the fuel tanks. Bolan reached through the window and managed to hit the ignition switch, killing the engine.

The Executioner opened the door to the rear compartment of the helicopter and was greeted by stacks and stacks of stainless-steel casks, each filled with enough prion-infected material to infect tens of thousands of cattle with bovine spongiform encephalopathy.

When he was certain the site was secured, he called Kurtzman on his sat phone. "Is the hazmat team on its way?" he asked.

"They'll be there within the hour, Striker," Kurtzman said.

"What's the status of the Ag Con facilities out west?"

"Both sites have been razed, and all the cattle in the Ag Con herd are being destroyed. We debriefed Rog, and we've got him leading teams of researchers out testing cattle in the surrounding herds, just to make certain there were no accidental infections in other populations."

"How's Rog doing?"

"Fair," Kurtzman said, "all things considered. He's in better shape than the Bowman woman."

"Is Kemp safe?"

"Yes, she's back at her home. She's asking about you, but no one's been able to answer her questions, since you don't officially exist."

"How about those technicians at the lab in the Killdeer Mountains?" Bolan asked.

"It turns out to be a very good thing that you didn't kill those boys, Striker. They've been a gold mine of information. It seems they weren't too happy about Chen leaving them for dead in the research lab."

"What did you find out?"

"Pretty much everything, including the names of Chen's accomplices, most of whom are holed up at the Ag Con facility in Ames. Able Team is on its way to Iowa to exterminate that rats' nest as we speak." Able Team was a crack commando team that Bolan had organized when he'd been directly involved with Stony Man Farm.

"That should ruffle some feathers on Capitol Hill," Bolan said. Ag Con had some of the most high-powered lobbyists in Washington, and they bought and sold members of congress the way kids used to trade bubblegum cards.

"It most certainly will, but Hal has cleared it with the Man," Kurtzman said, referring to the President. "Hal and the President are briefing select members of the Senate Intelligence Committee as we speak. Once they learn the nature of the threat we've just neutralized, it's a safe bet that there won't be a peep about all this from the Hill. There's not a member of congress who doesn't have a campaign fund that's not padded with Ag Con money. Whatever is left of Ag Con after Able Team is finished will be a shadow of its former self, with no political clout whatsoever. If they somehow remain in business, they'll have no choice but to fly straight."

"What about Dan Gould?" Bolan asked.

"That's between the two of you," Kurtzman said. "Handle that situation as you see fit."

Bolan pondered his options concerning Dan as he returned to the plane. He untied the man without saying a word.

Finally Dan broke the silence. "Now what?" he asked.

"Refuel the plane. We're going back to Watford City."

Once up in the air, Bolan said, "If you were me, what would you do about you?"

"What?" Dan asked.

"Think about it. If you were me, and you had the opportunity to rid the world of one more drug dealer, and no one on Earth would care about his disappearing, what would you do?"

Dan didn't answer.

"The reason I ask you this," Bolan said, "is because I'm giving you the option of making my decision for me."

"What?"

"You might want to expand your vocabulary," Bolan told Dan. "'What' is starting to get monotonous."

"What?"

"The way I see it, you've got two options," Bolan said. "Disband your drug operation and be satisfied with your legitimate business interests, or meet the same fate as your cousin and spend eternity in a shallow Badlands grave. You must make decent money from your car dealerships."

"It's not what it used to be, but yeah, I do all right."

"It seems to me that 'all right' is a major improvement over dead. Do you get what I'm saying?"

Dan seemed to be thinking over the Executioner's offer. Clearly he hadn't expected to live to see the sun rise one more time.

"Make no mistake," Bolan said. "If you choose to live, you will not have the option of going back into the business you and your deceased cousin operated. You so much as sell one gram of meth and I hear about it, I will hunt you down and I will kill you. You won't have to worry about legal fees, lawyers, or prisons, because I will be your judge, your jury and your executioner. And when I carry out the sentence, it won't be quick, clean and easy, the way it was for your cousin. If I have to come all the way back to western North Dakota to fulfill my promise, I'm going to make it as entertaining as possible. Do you understand?" Dan only nodded. Bolan had exaggerated on that last point. Though he would indeed make the return trip to remove an active drug dealer from the community, he would take no joy in doing so, and he would make the hit as quick and humane as possible. He just felt the slight exaggeration might give Gould extra incentive to walk the straight and narrow.

"Good. Now you're getting your first chance to prove yourself. I'm going to take a nap. Wake me up when we get to Watford City."

Don Pendleton's Mack Bolan

Kill Shot

**Homegrown radicals
seek global domination!**

The terror begins with ruthless precision
when the clock strikes noon, gunfire
ringing out in major cities along the East
Coast. At the heart of the conspiracy,
sworn enemies have joined for the nuclear
devastation of the Middle East. As blood
spills across the country, Bolan sights his
crosshairs on their nightmare agenda.

*Available June
wherever books are sold.*

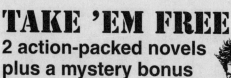

TAKE 'EM FREE
2 action-packed novels
plus a mystery bonus

NO RISK
NO OBLIGATION TO BUY

AleX Archer
TEAR OF THE GODS

The early chapters of history contain dangerous secrets…secrets that Annja Creed is about to unlock….

A dream leads archaeologist Annja Creed to an astonishing find in England—the Tear of the Gods. But someone knows exactly what this unusual torc means, and he will do anything to get his hands on it…even leave Annja for dead. Now she is fleeing for her life, not knowing the terrifying truth about the relic she risks everything to protect.

Available July wherever books are sold.

GOLD EAGLE®